Street Soldier

Street Soldier

Silhouettes

URBAN
BOOKS

www.urbanbooks.net

Urban Books, LLC
78 East Industry Court
Deer Park, NY 11729

ISBN 13: 978-1-60162-452-9
ISBN 10: 1-60162-452-2

First Printing June 2011
Printed in the United States of America

10 9 8 7 6 5 4 3 2 1

Distributed by Kensington Publishing Corp.
Submit Wholesale Orders to:
Kensington Publishing Corp.
C/O Penguin Group (USA) Inc.
Attention: Order Processing
405 Murray Hill Parkway
East Rutherford, NJ 07073-2316
Phone: 1-800-526-0275
Fax: 1-800-227-9604

Acknowledgments

First and foremost, thanks to God for ordering our steps. No matter what path You choose for us, we will be ready. To Urban Books, particularly Carl Weber, we appreciate the opportunity you've given us to share our talents with readers. To our agent and best friend in the whole wide world, Brenda Hampton, thank you for your years of support and guidance. We love you and you are truly the best!

To all of the Jamal "Prince" Perkinses of the world, we understand your struggles, but always know and recognize that you don't have to fall in line with what society deems you to be! There is a better life waiting for you to claim it!

4M2H
Silhouettes of a new generation . . .

Chapter 1

Yeah, I'm that nigga. Jamal "Prince" Perkins. You know, the one who makes you feel the need to lock your doors when I get closer and closer to your car. The one who makes the ladies grip their purse straps as I walk by. Or, the one who makes you walk in another direction only to avoid me. Yeah, I'm *that* one. I like putting fear in people everywhere I go, and it fucks me up when they think I don't trip off their actions. Trust me, if I wanted to get at you, I would. It depends on what kind of day I'm having, so consider yourself lucky if you don't find yourself being victimized by me.

For as long as I could remember, my life was like a battlefield. The Taliban and Al Qaeda were right around the corners, and fights in my hood happened almost every single day. Seven times out of ten, I was bumping fists with niggas who didn't know how to shut their mouths, or with fools who were hating on me. I'd always had this chip on my shoulder. At the age of seven, I wasn't playing with toy cars or building blocks. I wasn't eating dinner with my family at the table, or having father-to-son talks with my old dude. Fuck my deadbeat-ass father. I was hustling, trying to keep food in my mouth and clothes on my back by stealing shit and, sometimes selling weed. My homeboy kept me up on the game, and life was all about survival. A boy's best friend wasn't his dog around here; rather, it was a 9 mm he kept strapped to his side. Yeah, we were at war. With our own race and with anyone who dared to get in the way.

All I could say was some black folks were lucky, but, then again, many were not. You can't judge if you ain't been there. Thing is, if you get to know me you just may understand or like me. Like Lil Wayne said, "A nigga like me sometimes be misunderstood. It ain't about making excuses. This shit is the truth as I live it!"

I was in my first-hour class at North High School in the deep city of St. Louis, resting my banging head on the desk and trying my best to stay awake. I had been up all night, listening to my mom and her whack-ass boyfriend argue. I hated that fool, Raylo, and the two of us couldn't get along for nothing. He was on some kind of gangsta shit, trying to pimp my mama and impress her with shuffling a li'l crack cocaine around. The money he made wasn't much to brag about, but he paid most of the bills and helped put clothes on my back. Their constant arguments drove me crazy. My mama be bitching all the time, and I hadn't met a man yet who she hadn't argued with. I'd interfered with her arguments before, but it was a waste of my time. She always went back to her abusers, and when one of those fools stabbed me in the shoulder with a knife one day, that was it for me. I got myself a lifetime soldier mark, and every time I look at it, I think of my mama. Yeah, she kicked the nigga out, but he was back in less than two weeks. I had to face his ass every single day, knowing that he could have taken my life. That proved to me that my mama didn't give a damn about me, and from that moment on, I lost a lot of respect for her.

Sometimes I didn't even know why I went to school, and, for me, it was about getting free meals, seeing the dimes, and hanging with my boy, Romeo. We'd been down since the first grade and he was like a real brother to me. You rarely saw one of us without the other, but lately, things had changed. Romeo was into this new chick, Sabrina, and she had him wrapped around her finger. I didn't expect for that shit to last long, 'cause, like me, Romeo had a reputation for sticking and moving. He had that Chris Brown swagga going on, and I referred to him as my "mellow-yello." I gave his relationship with Sabrina two more weeks, and after that, she'd be history. Maybe by then, Romeo would have his head on straight and we could get back to what we did best—surviving.

I heard myself snoring, and when Mr. Betts shook my shoulder, I knew I was in trouble.

"What?" I said in a groggy tone, lifting my head from my desk.

"Sit up straight and wipe the dripping saliva from the corner of your mouth," he ordered.

Everyone in the classroom laughed loudly, including that trick, Nadine, who I had been on the phone with last night. How dare she laugh at me? I wiped the corner of my mouth with my shirt, and gave a hard stare at Nadine so she would silence herself.

"You'd better watch yourself," I spat. "And I wish the rest of y'all would shut the fuck up."

The classroom erupted with a bit more laughter. Mr. Betts's eyes cut me like a knife, but he kept quiet. Nadine's neck started to roll. "And if I don't shut up? What you gon' do, Prince? Hit me?"

Mr. Betts slammed a book on the floor, silencing everyone. "No more talking," he shouted. "Pay attention or get out!"

Nadine rolled her eyes, but I ignored her and focused on staying awake. My eyes were glued to the round, loud ticking clock on the wall. I watched the red second hand on the clock tick away, counting down how much time I had left in his class. Right on time, the loud bell rang and I rushed out of my seat to get to second hour. I couldn't wait to see my algebra teacher, Ms. Macklin, she was one bad-ass chick! I was only seventeen, but from the way she looked at me, I could tell she didn't care. Something about her made me feel close to her, and her seductive eyes were very addictive, like mine. Her body was like . . . damn! I dreamed about fuckin' her and could barely concentrate on my work. She was only twenty-six, and one of these days I was going to make her my wife. She put me in the mindset of Nicki Minaj, but she was sassy as Meagan Good. I loved to see her upset with the class and I did my best to seek her attention. She stayed on me, but deep down, I could feel there was more to it. Her eyes always connected with mine, and during my football games I could see her watching me. Yeah, she wanted me. And it would be just a matter of time before I showed her how much I wanted her too.

I tucked my wrinkly, outdated books underneath my arm, but before I made my exit Mr. Betts called my name.

"Come back into the classroom so I can speak to you for a minute," he said.

I sighed, knowing that I was about to catch some heat for my behavior. "Yes, sir," I said, slowly walking up to him and hanging my head down low. I kept my distance, as Mr. Betts's breath wasn't always right. He was an older black man, always preaching about doing the right things. Kinda had that James Earl Jones thing going on and his voice was stern as ever. He demanded respect, and, most of the time, he got it.

He lowered his silver-framed glasses, peering over them. A frown appeared on his face, causing it to wrinkle.

"Why are you always being disrespectful and napping in my class? I'm trying to teach you some important things about your history, and none of what I'm saying to you is sinking in."

Not intending to, I yawned. "I apologize, Mr. Betts, but I stayed up late last night watchin' my li'l cousin. My aunt didn't pick him up until three o'clock in the mornin', so I didn't get much sleep. Been kind of groggy, that's all."

"Was your mother at home?"

I thought of a quick lie. "Nah, she was at work. I got paid, so I really didn't trip."

Mr. Betts touched my shoulder and squeezed it. "You got a D on your chapter test. I know you can do better, Jamal, and I'd hate to see you get kicked off the football team because you can't make the grade. If you need some extra time to study, think about staying after school. I can help you, just like I help some of the other students around here."

I nodded, knowing damn well I wasn't about to stay after school. Six hours was enough, and if I couldn't learn what I needed to know then, too bad. Plus, I had practice after school. I wasn't going to trade in football practice for no tutoring bullshit, but I appreciated Mr. Betts's concerns.

"I'll let you know, Mr. Betts. But I gotta get to my next hour, or else I'll be late. Ms. Macklin is good for writin' niggas up for bein' tardy, so I'd betta get goin'."

Mr. Betts released my shoulder and pulled a notepad from his desk. The bell hadn't rung yet, but he gave me a pass to second hour, excusing my tardiness.

"Control your use of the word 'nigga.' It has some disturbing history tied to it, young man, and I never want to hear you use that word in my classroom again."

I took the note from Mr. Betts's hand and apologized again, this time for my choice of words. As soon as I left his classroom, I spotted my partna in crime, Romeo, at his locker. I boldly strutted my way through the noisy and crowded hallway, bumping shoulders with the fellas I didn't like and eyeballing the girls who couldn't keep their eyes off me. They say I resembled Trey Songz, and as much as I pumped iron, my body was uniquely cut like his, too. My thick braids were always neatly done, and the minimal, trimmed hair above my lip made me look sexy as ever. Yeah, I knew I was the shit, and there wasn't a nigga up in this mutha who could pull it off like me. Tattoos covered the muscles on my arms, and my mother's name, Shante, was inked on my chest. "Street Soldier" was tattooed up and down on it, too.

Romeo had his back turned, so he didn't see me coming. I poked my elbow in his back, getting his attention.

"What's up, nigga?" I laughed. We swiped our hands together, wiggling our fingers as well.

Romeo smiled, placing the stash of weed he had in his hand back into his locker. "Man, you scared the shit out of me. I thought you were the principal, Mr. King."

"Nah, but you'd better hide that shit. Before you do, give me one so I can go smoke that blunt in the bathroom."

Romeo peeked from left to right, then picked through a plastic bag for the thinnest tightly wrapped blunt he could find. "Here, man, I gotta get to class," he said, hurrying to close his locker. "Tell Ms. Macklin I said what's up, and give her my number so she can call me." Romeo grabbed his crotch and licked his lips.

We both laughed as he jogged down the almost empty hallway, trying to make it to his class. I stopped at my locker, retrieved my algebra book, and tucked it underneath my arm. Before going to class, I went into the piss-smelling bathroom and found myself an empty stall. I sat on the cracked, stained toilet seat and held the joint underneath my nose. The smell of pine trees hit me, so I knew what I was working with was good. After I lit it, I deeply inhaled, filling my lungs with smoke. I immediately felt the rush, and after I exhaled, I closed my eyes to feel the effects. I was at ease, and when a seed popped, I eased up on the joint. I glanced at my watch, realizing that I had already missed ten minutes of class. Time had flown by, and I knew Ms. Macklin would soon be wondering where I was. So, instead of finishing my festivities, I saved some for later. I wasn't too worried about the smell that had attached itself to my clothes, only because the smell of smoked blunts was always in the air. I left the bathroom, tossing my white hoodie over my head and dragging my feet down the hallway in my untied Jordan tennis shoes.

As I pulled on the heavy wooden door, Ms. Macklin was writing on the chalkboard and speaking to the class. When she saw me, her actions came to a halt and her eyes shot daggers. I laid the excuse note on her desk and made my way to the back of the class, saying not one word.

"Sit up front and pay attention," she snapped, facing the chalkboard. I turned around and searched for the closest seat I could find up front. It was in the last row, close by a window. Nadine's seat was behind it, and she was all smiles when she saw me take the seat in front of her.

I placed my book on the desk, and tuned in to Ms. Macklin's backside as it faced me. She wore a red pencil skirt that revealed no panty line whatsoever. Her black silk blouse tightened over her breasts, and the three-inch heels she wore made her look like a professional stripper. She was classy, though, and I liked that shit. Her caramel skin was flawless as ever, and the makeup on her face was a work of art. Through my eyes, she was perfect, and I went into a trance staring at her as she spoke. Moments later, she laid the chalk down and headed to her desk. She picked up the note and took another glance at me.

"Did you notice the time on this note, Jamal? I can't believe it took you almost fifteen minutes to get from one class to the next."

I scratched between my thick braids, contemplating a lie. "Mr. Betts gave me the pass, but he kept on talkin'. When you see him, you can ask him. He forgot to change the time."

Ms. Macklin ignored my comment and asked the class to clear our desks for a test. I had forgotten all about it, and I'd have been the first to admit that I didn't know what the hell was going to be on it. I watched as Ms. Macklin stood in front of each row, counting the number of papers for each student. When she got to my row, I sniffed her sweet-smelling perfume, and my eyes were glued to her perky breasts. Her hard nipples made my mouth water. I wanted to reach out my hands to grab them, but I had to be patient. I could feel it; my day was coming.

I passed the papers behind me and Nadine whispered my name.

"What?" I grumbled.

"Do you have an extra pencil I can use?"

"Hell, naw. Do I look like I got an extra pencil?"

"No, but you look high as hell. I can smell that shit all over you, and you know Ms. Macklin can smell it too."

I cocked my head back and frowned. "So fuckin' what? I do what the hell I wanna do, so shut up talkin' to me."

As the words left my mouth, Ms. Macklin came over to my desk. She swiped up my paper and set it on a table next to her desk.

"There's no talking during a test. Come sit up here and take your test, before I give you an F for discussing the answers."

Her suggestion was in my favor, so I smiled. I stood, pulling up my sagging jeans that revealed a portion of my gray boxer shorts. I sat as close as I could to Ms. Macklin and did my best to pretend that I knew what the hell I was doing. Surprisingly, I knew some of the answers without even studying or paying attention. In no way was I a dumb kid, but school just wasn't my forte. I was almost eighteen and was just a junior. I'd failed the eighth grade, because I had missed too many days of school. This school year, I had already missed eleven days and was falling behind. School had only been in session for three months, so that wasn't good. Today, however, I wanted to impress Ms. Macklin, so I threw myself into the test, giving it my all.

A half hour later, I was finished. Instead of turning in my test, I looked around the classroom and noticed the other students still working. Some of the students, however, were cheating their butts off, but Ms. Macklin hadn't noticed because she was busy grading papers. It was so easy to cheat, and that's why doing homework was such a waste of time. I often copied papers from other students, and many of us did what we had to do to get by. I'd said it before and I'd say it again: school was just for fun. The environment itself was all fucked up, and anytime you had to sit in the cafeteria and eat lunch with roaches, it was pretty bad. To me, we were treated like criminals. Every day, we were searched by security guards at the door, our bags were searched, and there was always someone with authority lurking around, trying to tell you what you couldn't do. The classrooms hadn't been updated since the 1960s, and covering the cracking paint on the walls with more paint just wasn't cutting it.

On some days, it was too damn hot in the classrooms to try to learn anything. The humidity made the walls look as if they had sweat running from them, and the fans in the windows weren't doing much but making the rooms hotter. By the end of the day, many of the students' clothes were sticking to their bodies, and the girls' hairdos were all fucked up. The hardwood floors were buckling, and the old desks that we sat in cramped my style. Graffiti was scribbled everywhere and we didn't even have the appropriate books to learn with. We had to share books all the time, and if that weren't enough, there were three people assigned to one rusty-ass locker. Nobody was to share shit with me, only because my locker was junky as hell and there wasn't enough room. Romeo was sharing his locker with Sabrina. She was in Ms. Macklin's class too, and when I looked up at Sabrina, she waved. I gave her a fake-ass grin. Simply put, I didn't like the bitch. She seemed sneaky and was always up in my business, trying to see what I was up to. I had to admit, though, that Romeo had himself a dime. She was smart and was the captain of the cheerleading squad. Her mother was a teacher at a nearby elementary school. She wasn't happy about her daughter hooking up with Romeo, but who cared? As far as I knew, Romeo hadn't hit it yet, and I was so sure that's why he was hanging on for as long as he had.

I placed my test on Ms. Macklin's desk. She picked it up to glance over it. Immediately following, she stood up and asked me to step out in the hall. I followed her, biting on my lip and agreeing with another boy in the class who had released a soft whistle.

Ms. Macklin halted her steps and folded her arms in front of her. "Craig, get back to taking your test. I'll be in the hall for a few minutes and I don't want any talking in here."

"Yes, ma'am," Craig said, lowering his head.

I stood outside of the door while Ms. Macklin stood in front of me with a mean mug. She looked pissed, and it messed me up how I could easily get her attention.

"Have you been smoking something?" she asked.

Like always, I knew my eyes were red as fire and it was obvious that I had been smoking. Still, I lied. "No, ma'am. I'm just tired, that's all."

"That's not the truth and you know it. If you are caught smoking anything in this school, you will be expelled. I suggest you think about your actions, Jamal, and get your act together. You're not focusing in class, and every time I look at you, you're drifting off somewhere. Why aren't you focusing in class?"

I shrugged, refusing to tell her the *real* reason why. "Like I said, I'm just tired. I don't get energized until fourth or fifth hour."

"Well, you need to start getting energized in my class. You've made some simple mistakes on your test and I want you to redo it."

"That ain't gon' happen. I'll make it up with extra credit or somethin', but I don't feel like retakin' that test."

She shook her head from side to side with disgust. "You will retake it, and I'm going to speak with the coach about your lack of participation in my class. If you can stay focused on the field, you can do so in class too."

"But it ain't like you're on the field."

She pursed her glossy, juicy lips. "What is that supposed to mean?"

I dropped my head, feeling that if she wanted the truth, then I would give it to her. After all, the truth was supposed to set you free, right? "I can't stay focused, ma, 'cause my thang be jumping out of my pants in your classroom. It can't contain itself, 'cause you fine as ever and—"

Ms. Macklin pointed down the hall. "I'm not your darn ma, and you need to go to the office, right now! You will not disrespect me. I am disgusted by your behavior."

I defensively held out my hands. "You asked me to tell the truth. Why I gotta get in trouble for tellin' the truth or for sayin' how I feel? My bad for offendin' you, but—"

"Go!" she yelled.

I bit my bottom lip, trying to prevent myself from going off. Instead, I flipped my hoodie over my head, eased my hands into my pockets, and slowly walked to the principal's office. It was already packed with students, so instead of waiting around to see Mr. King, I left. I knew I'd be in trouble, but what the hell. Two or three days of suspension would give me a chance to catch up on some of the sleep I'd been missing.

When I got home, my mama was sitting at the kitchen table smoking a Virginia Slim and counting a stack of crinkly, dirty dollars.

"Prince," she said, referring to me by my middle name. "What are you doin' home so early?"

"We had a half day," I said, looking into the empty refrigerator. "Why we ain't never got nothin' in this muthafucka to eat?"

"Why you ain't got no muthafuckin' job? If you want to eat, then go get a job. Don't be comin' up in here complainin' about what you ain't got. Raylo and me put nice-ass clothes on your back, and it wouldn't hurt for you to pitch in and take care of yourself."

I ignored my mama's comments. She was supposed to provide for me since I in no way, asked to be here. It was her responsibility to feed me, and even though she made sure that I had some of the finest clothes there were, I couldn't eat them. I slammed the refrigerator and headed off to my room. I closed the door, and fell back on my bed. My room was junky as hell, and it had been at least six months since my mama had been in here to clean it. I had a pile of clothes in one corner that needed to be washed, a trash can oozing over with trash was in another corner, and the musty smell could easily be toned down with Febreze. Still, my room was the only place where I could get peace of mind, and I rarely stayed anywhere else in our cramped two-bedroom house.

I reached for the football next to me and started tossing it in the air. I feared that Coach Johnson would cut me from the team, especially if he found out what had happened today. A part of me really didn't care, but then again, I did. I would miss all of the attention I got from playing, but more so all of the attention from girls. My phone stayed busy from them calling, but I really didn't have feelings for anybody. I guess I'd been too wrapped up with my thoughts of Ms. Macklin, but after today, she showed me that these feelings I had were not mutual. It was time to move on, I guessed, but I couldn't say that I was ready to give up.

I stayed in my room, trying to figure out how to get some money so I could get something to eat. I called Romeo's phone several times, but got no answer. Normally, his grandmother didn't have anything in the fridge to eat either, so that meant going to the corner store to stock up on a few items. It was a bit nippy outside, as the fall weather had just started to kick in. I put my hoodie over my head, tucked my Glock inside my pants, and eased my hands into my pockets. As I walked down Martin Luther King Boulevard, the first thing I saw was a prostitute approaching a white man in a car. She talked to him for a while, and soon after got inside of his car. He sped off into an alley, and a part of me couldn't blame her. Like me, I guess she felt the need to do whatever she had to do to get by.

Before I reached the corner store, I looked inside of a pawn shop's window, admiring the jewelry. One day I'd be able to go inside and buy whatever I wanted. There was a nice-ass platinum chain on display, and bling was everywhere. I could visualize that shit around my neck, and if they didn't have so much surveillance, I would bust inside and take what I wanted. Instead, I moseyed on down the street, making my way into the corner store.

As I entered, my eyes connected with the Arabian man behind the counter. He'd seen me in his store before, and always kept his eyes on me. I went up and down the aisles, licking my dry lips at everything I saw. My stomach growled at a package of Hostess Cupcakes and I held them in my hand. A bag of Hot Fries and a cold soda sounded pretty good too, so I searched for those, and then held them in my hands as well. My eyes turned to the Arabian man at the counter, and, as he was waiting on a customer, I put the soda in my pocket and tucked the cupcakes underneath my hoodie. I spotted a cold cut sandwich that I wanted, so I picked that up too. My eyes turned to the Arabian man again, but this time he waved for me to come up front.

"Are you finished?" he asked.

I cleared my throat and made my way to the counter. I put the Hot Fries and sandwich on the counter. He rang up my items, but I didn't have any money to pay. I patted my back pockets, pretending as if I'd lost my money.

"Damn," I said. "I thought I . . ."

The man stood stone-faced. Obviously, he knew I was bullshitting, so I made another move. I lifted the front of my hoodie, displaying my Glock.

"Don't start none, won't be none. I'll bring your money back to you tomorrow. As you can see, I'm runnin' a li'l short on change."

The Arabian man's eyes shifted to his side. I knew he kept his piece behind the counter, but his ass had to get to it.

I touched the top of my gun, implying that I would use it. "You don't want to lose your life over three fuckin' dollars, do you? I said I'd bring the money back to you tomorrow, nigga, now chill."

He said not one word. I swiped up the items on the counter and left the store. I wasn't sure if I was going to catch a bullet in my back, but if I was going to, I'd do so with a damn good sandwich in my mouth. By the time I got home, the sandwich was gone and so were the rest of the items I'd stolen. For me, this was an almost daily routine. I was running out of stores in my neighborhood to go to. In the past and, going forward, this was how things had to be for a street solider.

Chapter 2

Mama entered my room, spraying a can of Lysol in the air. With her house shoe she flattened a roach crawling up the wall, then smacked it on the floor. I was on the phone talking to Nadine while smoking my leftover blunt.

"This is ridiculous," Mama yelled while observing my room, particularly the provocative posters of naked black women I had on my wall. She hated the posters. "Boy, you need to get off that bed, put that joint aside, and clean up!"

Embarrassed by the unnecessary noise Mama was making, I hit the mute button.

"Why you all up in my room makin' that noise? Can't you see I'm on the phone?"

Mama snatched the phone from my hand and hung up on Nadine. She then took the last inch of my joint, placing it into her shirt pocket. She got high too, so I knew she'd use it for her purposes as well.

"Don't be smokin' my shit. But if you do, I must warn you, that shit is *fire.*" I laughed.

She slapped me on the back of my head, continuing to gripe about my room. "When are you goin' to do somethin' about this? How can you lay up in here like this?"

I stood up and picked up a pair of socks and underwear that were on my floor. "I'ma clean it up, but I thought you would hook it up for me. I tell you, as soon as I turned sixteen, you cut my ass off! No food, no cleanin', no nothin'."

Mama pointed her finger at me. "You damn right I did. You need to grow the fuck up, Prince, and learn how to take care of yourself. I'm not gon' be sniffin' behind your ass all my life, and I feel deeply sorry for the woman who has to live with you."

The phone rang and Mama got to it before I did. "He's not here," she yelled into the phone. "Call him back later!"

I hated when Mama got into my personal business. I stayed out of hers, and when she got into her li'l arguments, I turned up my music on my iPod to tune her out. My video games kept me occupied too, or I grabbed the phone to chat with some of the dimes in my classrooms. They all be trying to throw that pussy at me, especially since I was considered an outstanding athlete. I was the baddest running back North High School had ever had. My coach be on my ass about challenging myself, but I ain't feeling all of that. I liked playing football, but I ain't trying to make it no career.

I stood by my bed, wanting to curse Mama out for dissing the person who had just called. This is how we got along, so, at times, I didn't take her actions too personally. She made up my bed for me, then sat on the edge of it. Afterward, she lit the joint she'd put in her pocket and crossed her legs. It was customary for us to get down like that sometimes, smoking joints and drinking beers; we had been doing so since I was about thirteen. Mama had me when she was seventeen years old and she was still young at heart.

"This is some good shit," she spat while inhaling. "Where did you get this from?"

"From Romeo. I think he got it from his uncle."

"Is Romeo sellin' it?"

"Yes."

"Are you?"

"I was, but not anymore."

Mama took another hit from the joint, and then passed it back to me. "Raylo and me goin' out tonight. I'll be back later. Keep them bitches at a distance. I don't like them comin' to my house and I don't like them callin' here so much. That Nadine is workin' my nerves. I swear she calls here almost every ten minutes."

High as ever, I told Mama that I would correct Nadine for calling so much. But as soon as Mama and Raylo left, I called Nadine to come over. She was there within the hour, and, by then, my room had been tidied and the Lysol was working its magic. She'd bought me some McDonald's, and I sat on the bed, chomping down on my saucy Big Mac and licking the salt from the fries off my fingers.

"Boy, slow down," Nadine said, standing in front of my dresser. "You gon' choke yourself."

I wiped my mouth with my hand, and within minutes, I was finished. I tossed the bag in the trash and sat against the headboard with my shirt off.

"Why you way over there, ma?" I asked Nadine. "You can sit on my bed. I promise you that I won't bite."

Nadine laughed and carefully eased onto my bed. She wore a purple sweat suit and clean white Nike tennis shoes. Her hair was neatly combed back, but flipped at the ends. She was definitely my flava and resembled Raven-Symoné. Even so, I was out for one thing, and one thing only.

"You know you gon' be in trouble tomorrow for leaving school, don't you?" she said.

I shrugged. "I predict that I will be, but oh well. Did Ms. Macklin say anything about me after I left?"

"Nope, but I heard her on the phone, talking to another teacher. She mentioned your name, but I can't really say what they were talking about."

The phone rang, and when I looked to see who it was, I saw that it was another girl from school who I had given my number to. I'd already gotten into those panties, so I ignored the call. Instead, I scooted down on the bed, moving closer to Nadine. We had been spending an enormous amount of time on the phone, and it was time for her to put up or shut up. As she sat next to me, I lay back with my hands behind my head, looking up at the ceiling. Nadine leaned over me and used her fingers to trace my mother's name tattooed on my chest.

"Who is Shante?" she asked.

"My mother."

"Why you got tats all on your arms like that? I like how you got 'Street Soldier' tatted north to south on your chest. That's dope, and I saw the same thing on Romeo. Y'all think y'all ballers or something?"

"I am a baller. Don't nobody run that ball like me, and you know that. Besides, I like my tats. Are you sayin' you don't like the other ones?"

"Oh, I love them. I think they hooked up. I was just asking."

"Can I ask you somethin' then?" I asked. Nadine nodded. "Can I have a kiss?"

She smiled, then leaned in closer to me so we could kiss. As far as I was concerned, I was a good kisser. Nadine, though, wasn't. Like always, I worked with what I had, and when I tried to unzip her jacket, she stopped me.

"What are you doing?" she asked.

I sighed. She knew damn well what I was getting to. "What does it look like?"

She slowly sat up, gripping the top of her jacket. "I . . . I need to tell you something, Prince."

I could feel the bullshit coming down. "What?"

"I didn't come over here to have sex with you."

I quickly sat up. "Then what did you come over here for? You knew what I wanted, didn't you?"

She swallowed and lowered her eyes to the ground. "Yes, but I wanted to wait for that. I thought that we could hook up as boyfriend and girlfriend, then sex between us would happen." She looked at me. "Besides, I'm a virgin and I wanted my first time to be with someone special."

"What in the hell do you think this is? We've been talkin' on the phone for weeks, ma. I thought you were down with this, and if you prefer that we're boyfriend and girlfriend, then cool. Now what?"

"Are you serious? Don't be playing with me, boy, just so you can get some."

I stood up and stretched. Nadine's eyes were all over my chiseled body, but I could tell she needed to be a bit more persuaded.

"Look," I said. "This ain't no game, baby. I'm with you on this, and all it is is sex. We don't have to commit ourselves just because we're havin' sex, do we?"

Nadine rolled her big, round, pretty eyes. "I'm not saying all of that, but I want to get something out of this, Prince. I see how you do them other girls, and I want things to be different between you and me."

I kneeled down in front of her, touching her hands to make her comfortable. "Things with us will be different. I ain't feelin' those other girls, but I like the hell out of you. Come on, take your clothes off, all right?"

"What about Ms. Macklin? I see how you be looking at her, and that shit drives me crazy."

"Please. I have a crush on Ms. Macklin, but that woman ain't thinkin' about me. I know you ain't trippin' off her, are you?"

Nadine looked down again and fumbled with her fingernails. I could tell she was nervous, but I was anxious. "Please," I begged.

She hesitated, then answered. "Go turn off the lights."

"For what? Don't you want to see me in action?"

She chuckled, then slightly pushed my shoulder. "I'm sure I'll feel you and that's enough. If I tell you to stop, Prince, then you'd better do it. Now, go turn off the lights so I can get undressed."

Just for the hell of it, I gave Nadine a lengthy kiss and turned off the lights. My tiny room was pitch-black. I removed my jeans and underwear, and waited on the bed until I felt Nadine's thick, naked body on top of mine.

"Do you have any condoms?" she whispered.

"No, I don't. I gotta get to the store to get some, but I don't have time to go get them right now. I swear I'll have one next time, and when I bust this nut, I'll pull out, okay?"

Nadine didn't say a word. Our tongues intertwined and my hands roamed her curvaceous body. She was stacked and my dick couldn't help but jump to get at her. I laid her back on the squeaky, spring-filled mattress, and positioned myself to enter her. I barely cracked her code before she started complaining.

"Easy, Prince," she groaned. "Go real, real slow."

I did my best to take it easy, but seeing Nadine's light-colored breasts bounce around in the dark turned me on. Her goods were nearly suffocating my thang, but the warmth and tightness of her insides made me want to cum fast. Controlling myself a bit longer was a mind thing, but, for now, my mind was telling me to come inside of this trick and save the rest for another day.

Nadine managed to handle the semi-beating I'd put on her pussy, and it cooled down when my sperm swam inside of her. The fifteen minutes that she'd remember for the rest of her life were now over, but our time together meant nothing to me. I couldn't count how many virgins I'd been into, and had lost count of the girls I'd had sex with. They made this shit too easy, and it was pretty cool to get sex when I wanted it, how I wanted it, and where I wanted it. After today, I was sure Nadine would accommodate any future needs I would have, and the way she'd cut up throughout our short time together implied just that.

Afterward, I got up to crack a window, trying to drown out the smell of sweaty sex. We lay in bed, listening to Lil Wayne spill his lyrics over the radio.

"Did you enjoy yourself?" I asked.

Nadine nodded with glee in her eyes. My sheets were up to her breasts, and she kept them covered so I wouldn't see them.

"It's still dark in here so why are you hidin'?" I asked.

"I don't know." She removed the sheets and moved in closer to me. Her head rested on my arm, and we were both pretty comfortable.

"How long are you goin' to stay?" I asked. "It's gettin' late, and I know your mama might start lookin' for you."

"I told her I was spending the night at a friend's house. When I leave, I'm going to her house. You ain't ready for me to leave already, are you?"

Deep down, yes, I was. I wanted my bed to myself, and I had phone calls to return. I hadn't spoken to Romeo all day, and, besides that, Mama told me not to invite anyone over. I still hadn't played my new game on PS3, and now that I had been *refreshed*, I got out of bed to play.

Nadine remained in my bed, I guessed hoping for seconds. I had gotten so indulged by my game that I almost forgot she was there. That was, until Mama opened the door; her mouth hung open and she stared at me like I was crazy. I could tell she was fucked up; the glassy look in her eyes said so. She eyeballed Nadine on my bed, but lucky for me, I was sitting on the floor.

"Hello, Ms. Perkins," Nadine said.

Mama ignored her. She came into the room, handing me a bag of fried rice from the Fried Rice Kitchen in Wellston, and a forty-ounce can of Miller beer to quench my thirst.

"Thanks," I said, taking the beer. "I already ate, though. Can you put the bag in the fridge for me so I can eat it tomorrow?"

Mama ignored me and left the room. I knew she was tripping because Nadine was there, so I asked her to leave. Relieved, I watched as she put her clothes on and left without putting up a fuss.

The next day, I was in big trouble. Right before first hour, I was standing at Romeo's locker, whispering to him about what had happened between Nadine and me. He told me that he and Sabrina had gotten into an argument last night, and said he'd spent the night on the phone, trying to make up with her. That's why he hadn't called me. Just as he was apologizing, Mr. King gripped the back of my neck and ordered me to his office. I hated that he was embarrassing me; as we walked through the hallway to get to his office, all eyes were on us. People were whispering, or, if not, they were laughing. I kept my cool and sat in front of Mr. King's desk to explain my abrupt departure from school yesterday.

"My bad, Mr. King, but as I was waitin' in your office, I called home to check on my mother. She was cryin' and I figured she and her boyfriend had been scrappin'. I rushed home to see what was up. I wasn't thinkin' straight, but I knew that I had to get home fast."

Mr. King sat across from me with his hands clenched together. I could hear the heavy breathing coming from his huge flared nostrils, and the intimidating look on his face said that he didn't believe me.

"What in the hell am I going to do with a student like you, Jamal?" He opened a folder that had my name written on a label. He looked through some papers, shaking his head in disbelief. "Your grades are sinking, you're skipping class, you're around here smoking weed, and you're sexually harassing my teachers. Then, on the bright side, you're good at playing football, you're polite to *some* teachers, and many of the kids at this school like you."

"I can always bring up my grades, Mr. King, but I take offense to you sayin' I'm around here sexually harassin' teachers. If that's the case, Ms. Macklin is harassing me. She around here dressin' all sexy and shi . . . stuff, and I'll be the first to admit that my testosterone levels keep me horny. Why should I be punished when she's the one who asked me to tell her the truth? It's not fair, and somethin' about the whole thing just don't seem right to me."

Mr. King rubbed the top of his bald head. "Boy, what do you know about testosterone levels?" He chuckled. He then called for his secretary to buzz Ms. Macklin into his office. Five minutes later, she came in and closed the door behind her.

"Yes, Mr. King," she said. "Did you call for me?"

Mr. King put on a big, bright smile, and the look in his lustful eyes implied that his testosterone levels were kicking it up too. How could they not, as once again Ms. Macklin was dressed to impress in gray pants and a button-down light pink shirt that squeezed her melon breasts. She looked a bit more conservative than usual, but if I'd had a pole, I'd have placed it right in front of her, just to watch her go to work.

Not intending to, I licked my lips, attempting to catch the liquids forming in my mouth. Ms. Macklin, however, never looked my way, and gave her attention to Mr. King.

"What do you suggest that I do with this young man?" he asked.

Looking pretty as ever, she swiped the long bangs away from her forehead, and folded her arms. "You're the principal, but I would like for him to be assigned four to eight hours of detention. Maybe he'll use that time to study, and, hopefully, he'll think hard about what he said to me. I won't stand for it, Mr. King, and Jamal knows better."

My mouth hung wide open. "Four to eight hours! Come on, ma . . . Ms. Macklin, you trippin'. If I miss any more practices, Coach Johnson gon' bench me. We playin' those white boys this weekend and I gotta play in that game."

She threw her hand back. "I don't care anything about a football game. You need to get your act together, and from my understanding, you'll be kicked off the team if you don't bring up your grades."

"She's right," Mr. King added. "And I think detention will do just fine. Starting today, you can do two hours after school until the eight hours are completed. Bring plenty of study materials, and I think you owe Ms. Macklin an apology."

I was mad as hell. I started to tell both of them to go to hell, but that would have made matters worse. Instead, I cut my eyes and told Ms. Macklin, again, that I was sorry for what I'd said.

"If you can't handle being in my classroom, Jamal, then maybe Mr. King should consider moving you to another class. My job is to teach, not to play around with you like these girls around here do. As long as you understand that, I think we'll be fine."

I kept my mouth shut, upset that Ms. Macklin was putting on a front. Deep inside I felt that she liked me, but I understood that she had to play it cool in front of Mr. King. He was suckered by her presence; I watched as he eyeballed her backside when she left his office. I started to call him on his shit, but what good was that going to do me? He'd deny it, and I'd get more hours of detention thrown at me. He wrote out my detention slip and asked me to sign it.

"This says only four hours. I thought you said eight."

He winked. "Do your four hours, Jamal, and be done with it. Don't say a word to anyone, but you'd better not be sent to my office again. In the meantime, I'll talk to Coach Johnson about the game on Saturday and see what I can do to get you to play."

I smiled and quickly signed the detention slip.

When I got to Ms. Macklin's class the next day, I kept quiet. She walked up and down the aisles, returning the test we had taken yesterday. I got a 70 percent and was content with it. She acted as if I had done so poorly, but I guess her face was cracked when she saw I hadn't done too badly. As she started to review the answers, Nadine tapped my back and handed me a piece of paper. I opened it and it read, CAN I COME OVER TONIGHT?

I jotted down, MAYBE, BUT WHAT WE GON' DO, MA?

I secretly gave the folded paper back to her. A few minutes later, she returned it to me. It read, WE'RE GO-ING TO HAVE SEX AGAIN, THAT'S IF YOU AIN'T TOO TIRED.

I replied, SOUNDS INTERESTING TO ME. CAN I INSTRUCT YOU ON HOW TO SUCK MY DICK?

I gave the paper back to Nadine and she laughed out loudly. Ms. Macklin turned her attention to us.

"Nadine, since you're interrupting my class, why don't you come up here and teach it. Bring that note in your hand up here, and share it with the class. I'd be interested in finding out why this piece of paper is so important that you and Jamal can't pay attention to me reviewing the test."

At first, I was slumped down in my chair, but I quickly sat up. Nadine attempted to get out of the situation, but Ms. Macklin ordered her up front. The students in the classroom were cracking up, especially when I raised my hand and asked Ms. Macklin if I could leave to go to the restroom.

"No," she said, turning her attention to Nadine, who stood embarrassed as hell. "Now, go ahead, Nadine. Read what's on the paper. If you don't, I will."

Nadine swallowed the lump in her throat and looked over at me. At this point, everybody knew what the hell I was about, so I really wasn't embarrassed.

"Can . . . can I come over tonight?" Nadine stuttered. "Maybe, but what we gon' do, ma? We're going to have, uh . . . have you-know-what again, that's if you ain't too tired."

The students cracked up, and a girl, Antonette, who I'd had a quickie with before, was pursing her lips and whispering, "Trifling."

"Sounds interesting to me," Nadine continued. "Can I instruct you on how to suck my D?"

Some of the boys fell out on the floor, laughing so hard. The girls were shaking their heads, and Ms. Macklin stood up. "Quiet," she yelled, as Nadine took her seat.

"Nadine and Jamal, if you think this is a sex education class, you're in the wrong place. Save the poetry for another time, and do not pass any more notes in my classroom. As a matter of fact," she said, pulling back the chair at a table that sat next to her desk, "Jamal, make this your permanent seat. I need to keep my eyes on you, and I want to make sure you don't get into any more trouble."

I pretended to be upset, but having a permanent seat next to Ms. Macklin was fine by me!

Chapter 3

The football game was close—twenty-one to seven-teen. I couldn't believe that we were losing to West High School, but going against cocky white boys was tough. Our whole team was black, and so were our cheerleaders. Earlier, I fucked up and fumbled the ball on the twenty-yard line. The two touchdowns I'd made helped me feel good, but there was nothing exciting about being down four points.

For whatever reason, I guess I wasn't taking the game seriously enough. I'd stayed up last night rocking Nadine's goodness to sleep. She wore my jersey to the game, and the continuous female distractions in the stands caused me to lose focus. She was flaunting her-self around, and I saw her and one of the other chicks in my classroom arguing about something. In addition to that, West High had a cold-ass black cheerleader named Monesha. She was a dark buttered brown, and had slanted catlike eyes that melted a nigga's heart. Her smile threw me off, and I fumbled the ball again!

"What in the hell is wrong with you?" Coach Johnson spat, looking angry, like rapper Ice Cube with a goatee. I walked off the field. West High had recovered the ball and I was pissed. "Get your head on straight, fool! If not, stay on the goddamn bench!" Coach said.

Coach Johnson took football too seriously. I didn't mind getting cussed out by him, but his words didn't encourage me to step up my game. What did, though, was when one of the players from West High started talking shit to Romeo, who was a defensive tackle. The player slipped right through Romeo's arms and laughed about it. Romeo removed his helmet and came over to the sidelines, because Coach Johnson had pulled him out of the game.

"Man, this some bullshit," Romeo said with a heaving chest. "Them white boys be playin' dirty. The referees ain't being fair, and didn't you see number twenty-four jump offside?"

I nodded, and after three plays, West High was out. It was our turn again, and I waited for Coach Johnson to put me in the game. On the first down, he didn't.

"Come on, Coach Johnson," I said, following him along the sideline. "Let me back in the game."

"Get that damn butter off your fingers and I will. That's some serious shit out there, Jamal, and this team don't have time for you to be out there playing like a Girl Scout."

"I ain't playin', all right? Let me back in the game, and I promise you a touchdown. Besides, I owe it to you."

Coach Johnson looked at me and cut his eyes. He yelled for the other running back to come out, and put me in.

Waiting for the play to begin, I stood behind the quarterback and eyeballed West High's defensive line. Those white boys were hungry for some black meat. Sweat dripped from their foreheads and their faces were lined with wrinkles. Their teeth were gritted, and it seemed as if every last one of them was growling at me. I took a quick glance at Monesha, but she was busy kicking her legs up high. My train of thought left me for a minute, and before I knew it, the quarterback tossed the football into my hands. After gaining one yard, I was stood straight up and slammed to the ground by a player weighing way over 250 pounds. My head was spinning, as I only weighed about 180 pounds. The crowd booed, and my back was hurting like hell. I felt as if I couldn't move. I blinked my eyes to clear them, only to see one of West High's defensive players standing over me.

"You ain't shit. Get yo' weak punk ass up." He pounded his chest and walked away.

This muthasucker was sounding like my mama. That was the last thing he should have done; his words pumped fire into my heart. I jumped to my feet, and when I looked over at Coach Johnson, he was shaking his head.

"Come on now, Jamal!" he yelled. "Get your shit to-gether!"

I was trying, but damn. These white boys were strong as hell, and I knew that in order to overpower them, my strength had to come from within. So, for the next play, I got mad. I thought about my deadbeat-ass father, who I saw every now and then on the streets, but never spoke to me. Then my thoughts turned to my whack-ass mama, and the many nights I'd lost sleep from listening to her get her ass kicked. I thought about the overcharging sly-ass Arabian man at the corner store, and the black couple sitting in their car yesterday who I'd robbed. The black man had tried to get gangsta, but his braveness got him smacked across the face with my Glock. His woman spit in my fucking face, and I ain't never slapped a bitch so hard in my life. He managed to drive off, and even though I wanted to take a shot at his ass, I didn't. My stomach was still growling from hunger pains, and since that nigga Romeo been tied up with that trick Sabrina, I felt as if I was in this world alone! Yeah, I was mad. Now,

I was mad as hell! I was too young for this shit, and it felt as if the world had been resting on my shoulders.

The quarterback slammed the ball into my midsection, and I let loose. I bolted down the field, feeling like a tiger, roaring through the crowd and knocking down everyone in my way. All I could hear was the screaming crowd yelling, "Prince," and telling me to go. At the nineteen-yard line, I was tackled from behind, but that was after a gain of forty-five yards.

I hurried to my feet and threw the ball to the ground, spiking it. I purposely jogged by the white boy who had stood over me talking shit. "Who the weak muthafucka now, nigga? It's time to get this shit on the road." I bumped his shoulder, and the referee threw up his yellow flag. My personal foul set us back fifteen yards, and Coach Johnson was livid.

"Wise up, Jamal! They playin' you, man. Playin' you like a fiddle. Get it done this time! We got two minutes left in the game and it's time to step up or step out!"

I looked at the coach and nodded. This time, though, my eyes slipped to Ms. Macklin in the stands, who was on her feet. I could see her smiling at me from a distance, and that made me feel good. The next down was for her, and when I gained back the fifteen yards from the foul, I felt even better. Still, it was third down and I didn't need a first down, I needed a touchdown. The bilateral pass came my way, but before I could catch it, a defensive player from West High stepped in and intercepted the ball. He swiftly ran down the field, and even though I tackled him from behind, they were now on the verge of making another touchdown.

My spirits were crushed and feelings were bruised. Coach Johnson was mad as hell, but more so disappointed. As the seconds wound down on the clock, my stomach turned in knots. I had the audacity to pray for God to turn things around, but He obviously didn't hear my call. The ten-second countdown came, and before I knew it, the game was over. The people on West High's side were on their feet, jumping for joy. This was a bad-ass feeling. The white boy who I'd scuffled with throughout the game had the nerve to walk over to me and hold out his hand.

"Good game," he said, then patted me on the back twice.

I shook his hand. As I walked off the field, the girls from our school were chanting, "Prince."

"Good game, Prince," they said. "You still the best!"

My head stayed low. If it hadn't been for those damn girls, maybe I would have played better. That went for Ms. Macklin too, and as soon as I started thinking about her, things went downhill. I cracked my knuckles from frustration, and that's when I saw Romeo run to catch up with me. "We should have won that fuckin' game. The refs were bullshittin', man, and them white boys wasn't shit."

"Yeah, I know. But a win is a win, no matter how you look at it."

"I agree. But, uh, what up for tonight?"

"Not a damn thing. I take it you have plans with Sabrina, right?"

"I did, but I'm gon' cancel. I need to move some of these herbs my uncle gave me and I want you to go with me. I'll hit you with a li'l somethin'-somethin', so be ready by eight."

I didn't feel up to slinging no weed with Romeo tonight, but I damn sure needed some money. We headed to the locker room with the rest of the players, but before going inside, someone touched my shoulder. I turned to see who it was.

"Good game, Jamal. You know you weren't supposed to be playing today, but like always, you made the game very exciting. Keep up the good work," Ms. Macklin said.

She sashayed away, and I couldn't help but think she was flirting with me. Her eyes said it all, and so did those tight jeans she wore that plumped her ass up just right. *Damn*, I thought. *When, where, and how am I ever going to hit that?*

I walked into the house, only to find my mama sitting in the living room. She looked like a zoned-out Diana Ross from the movie *Lady Sings the Blues*. Her natural hair sat high on her head like an afro and her bugged eyes were red as ever. As far as I knew, she didn't smoke crack, but remnants from the joint were in an ashtray. As I got closer to her, I could see the bruise underneath her eye. I lifted her face with my hand and shook my head.

"It looks painful. Did Raylo do that to you?"

She smacked my hand away. "Nah, nigga, now keep your dirty hands off my face. And please, please go in there and take a shower. With that football uniform on, you got my house stankin'."

I looked deep into my mama's eyes, not sure if I really loved her. Since I'd been playing football, I'd asked her to come to my games, but she never, ever showed. Then there were times that I felt as if she cared. She used to keep my room clean, cook for me sometimes, talk to me in a better tone, and invite me to watch movies with her. She often inquired about my day, and sometimes bought me books so that I could read. Things were different now, and I didn't know who she was or what she was becoming. Like all of the men in her life, preferably older men, Raylo had her so fucked up. It was becoming obvious that she didn't have time for me.

"We lost our game today. I made two touchdowns, though. The other team was good and the white boys were *way* bigger and stronger than us. You should have seen them."

"I'm sure they were. You need to stop wastin' your time with that mess, and if you don't remember nothin' I tell you, you can be sure of this: The white man gon' always be better than us, simply because that's just the way it is. They control the universe. Even if you make it to the NFL, they gon' write those checks for you. They can cut your black butt off when they want to. Look at how they did Mike Vick. It's a shame. I don't want you gettin' all hyped about some shit that may not ever happen. As a matter of fact, don't even talk to me about it because I don't want to hear it. I worked my fingers to the bone, cooking and cleaning for a white man for years. Time his money came up missing, he blamed me and threw my ass out. Called me all kinds of niggas, only to find out it was his son who stole the money. That muthafucka still ain't apologized to me, and after all of the ass wiping I did for his old tail, it left a bad taste in my mouth about these white folks out here. Don't you get caught up in that mess. I mean it."

I stood stone-faced, wiping the fine hair above my lip. Nah, I didn't like her ass, but at the end of the day, she was my mama. "Thanks for the inspiration," was all I could say, and walked away.

I heard Romeo blowing his horn, so I jetted outside so we could go. Nadine and some of the other chicks from school had been blowing up the phone, trying to see what I was getting into tonight. Thus far, the only plan I had was hanging out with Romeo, but, as always, our plans were destined to change. I hopped into the front seat of his black and gold 1980s Impala and he sped off. The tailpipe was nearly hanging to the ground and we could hear it scraping the concrete. His burgundy leather interior was okay, but it had a few rips in it where you could see the foam cushion. The Impala got Romeo from point A to B, and since I didn't have a car at all, I couldn't complain. Jay-Z's lyrics spilt from the loud, thumping speakers, and we rapped right along with him. Romeo already had a joint wrapped tight, and it wasn't long before we pulled his car over and took a few hits.

"So, my nigga," he said, passing the joint back to me, "after I drop off these two packages, where to?"

"They been hollerin' about this party at the Region's Hall on Twentieth Street all week. We goin' or what?"

"Fa'sho," Romeo said. He started his car, and after making his deliveries, we headed to the Region's Hall. While in the car, Romeo reached in his pocket and gave me $200.

"I know I've been busy lately, but I hope there ain't no hard feelings. Sabrina takin' up a lot of my time, but as soon as I feel the hot pocket, things gon' be different."

"She still holdin' out on you? I can't believe that."

"I can't either. But if I done came this far, I may as well hang in there."

"Hey, whatever. I don't think I could wait that long. She playin' games, man, and you need to let her game backfire."

Romeo inhaled, swallowing the smoke from the joint. "I agree." He squinted from the rush. "If she ain't upped it in two more weeks, I'm done."

I slapped his hand against mine, and we wiggled our fingers. I then tucked the $200 in my pocket and thanked him.

"At last, I can go get me some groceries. I'm gon' buy me some new tennis shoes, too, and if you ain't doin' nothin' this Sunday, come pick me up so we can hit the flea market on Rock Road."

Romeo nodded, and after finishing two blunts, we made our way to the hall.

The Region's Hall was packed with a mixture of high school students from all over St. Louis. Surprisingly, everyone seemed to be getting along. I noticed some of the white boys from the game earlier, and when I saw the one who stood me up straight a few times, I made my way over to him. I tugged at my hanging jeans, and was looking fly in my white Ed Hardy designer shirt with skeletons. It poured over my muscles, and the fake bling around my neck had a lot of heads turning. My fresh braids had a shine, and thanks to my mixed grandmama for the naturally curly hair, I looked original and felt spectacular.

The players from the team saw me coming their way. Romeo stayed behind, talking to some joker from another school, but I didn't know him. Just to break the ice, I held out my hand, and the player from the other team stepped forward to shake my hand.

"Hey, brotha, what's up?" he said.

"Shit. Just wanted to say hello and congratulate you fools on a good win."

The white boy patted my back. "Yeah, but you guys played a damn good game. You were runnin' on me like Usain Bolt or somethin'. I was out there havin' a heart attack tryin' to keep up with yo' ass."

They all laughed and so did I. We stood around talking about the game and going off on the referees. Even they admitted the refs weren't being fair. As I indulged in my conversation, I noticed Nadine dancing with a white boy from another school. I didn't care that she was dancing with anyone, but the trick had the nerve to have on my jersey. It was bad enough she had been flaunting herself around at the game, but couldn't she have changed clothes before she came to the party? That shit didn't sit right with me, and I quickly wrapped up my exchange with the fellas. With my hands in my pockets, I swaggered my way to the dance floor, only to be pulled by my arm and stopped in my tracks.

"Why you moving so fast?" Monesha said, yelling over the blasting hip-hop music. A wide smile covered her face, and her hazel eyes were piercing my heart. "Do you wanna dance?"

I got a quick glimpse of the flimsy ruffled orange skirt she wore, and her dark-chocolate, oily toned legs underneath. Dancing, of course, was not what I wanted to do.

"Wait right here, ma," I suggested. "I don't feel like dancin', but I'll be back in a few minutes."

She took her hand off my arm and I walked away. My pace was fast, and when I stepped up to Nadine she looked surprised to see me. She was giddy as ever, and threw her arms around me to give me a hug.

"Hey, Boo," she said, looking and smelling as if she had been drinking.

I removed her arms from around me. "Why you got on my jersey? You got fifteen minutes to find somethin' else to put on, or else."

She stumbled backward. "Why you trippin'? I've had this thing on all day, boy, so stop playing."

Irritated by her, and by the fact that she had let another person rub on her booty, I grabbed her face, squeezing her cheeks in my hand. "Don't play with me, girl, all right? Go take that muthafucka off and give it to me before the end of the night."

Everyone looked as I shoved her face back and stormed away. I strolled by Monesha, but nudged my head to the side so she could follow me.

Romeo had given me the keys to his car, and Monesha and I were in the backseat slapping near-naked bodies. I had her skirt flipped up from the back while she was kneeled over on the seat. The loud sounds of my thighs smacking her backside hard echoed in the car, and so did our moans and groans. Monesha had mad skills. When she turned on her back, I toyed with her wetness, leaning in to kiss her.

"Dis some good-ass shit, girl. You got my ass about to cum, big time."

"Do it. Pop my cherry wide open," she said, grinding on me raw. By the feel of her wide insides, I could tell she was far from being a virgin.

Monesha pulled her button-down shirt aside, exposing her dark, thick, chocolate nipple. Her breast was the prettiest thing I'd ever seen, and before I let loose, I lowered my head to suck it.

"*Damn,*" she shouted. "Work it, Prince. Who would have thought you could work it like this?"

I really couldn't, but since Monesha was proving herself to be all that, I stepped up my game. I dipped into her insides like I was stirring a pot of hot and creamy soup. It was delicious, and it caused one hell of an explosion. The car was lit up with the smell of erotic sex, and, yes, this was a moment I wasn't going to forget anytime soon. Monesha cleaned me up with her mouth, and it was a good thing that, this time, I didn't have to ask for head.

As soon as we got back inside, Romeo tried to warn me that Nadine was on a rampage. According to him, she'd seen his car rocking and knew that I had left the Hall with Monesha. Before I could get out a word, she came up from behind, screaming loudly and doing what I hated the most—embarrassing me. Tears welled in her eyes.

"Where in the hell have you been, Prince, and don't lie! I saw you leaving with her!" Nadine's eyes scolded Monesha as she saw us walk in together. Monesha ignored her and walked away.

I pointed to my chest. "Are you yellin' or talkin' to me, ma? I don't respond to that kind of noise. You'd better check yourself for comin' at me like a hood rat."

Romeo turned to walk away, and I followed him. People were looking in our direction, and that's when I turned around to see what was behind me. Nadine had a bat in her hand, and as she came down with it, it almost cracked me upside my head. I ducked out of the way and grabbed the bat with my hand.

"You crazy-ass bitch!" I yelled. I took the bat away from her and shoved her backward. Romeo tried to hold me back, but Nadine had gone too far. She'd asked for it, and only because she was still wearing my jersey, I grabbed her by her arm and shoved her outside. Romeo was still trying to calm me, but I yelled for him to leave me the fuck alone.

"This stupid-ass girl is trippin'," I said in anger with spit flying from my mouth. "Now, take off my damn jersey before I rip that muthafucka off of you!"

Nadine wanted to play tough, but doing so with me wasn't the right move. She lunged out at me, and my fist caught her right in her jaw. That surely calmed her ass down, and when she dropped to the ground, Romeo yelled for us to go.

"Man, with all these people lookin', somebody gon' call the police. Let's go!"

I was too mad to go. Nadine had taken me to a place I promised myself I would never go, especially after seeing Mama get beat down for many, many years. My pride was hurt, though, and Nadine had driven me to my limit.

"Take off my fuckin' jersey!" I yelled.

She sat on the ground sobbing, while holding her hands over her face. "I ain't doing nothing," she challenged.

Romeo ran off to get his car, and that's when I grabbed my shirt, attempting to pull it off Nadine's back. We tussled, and her struggles caused me to punch her again. This time, I drew blood from her lip. I heard a door behind me open, and when the white boy she was dancing with came outside, he pulled Nadine away from me.

He had a bewildered look on his face. "Dude, chill with that shit, all right?"

Mama's words rang out in my head. *White people always gon' be better than us and they're in control of the universe. Nigga, when will you ever learn?*

Before I knew it, I was all over the white boy, slamming bone-crushing blows anywhere they could land. He should have known better than to interfere with my business, and I knew now that he had wished like hell he hadn't come outside. Some of his friends, including the player I had reconciled with, had come outside to see what was up.

"Stop the madness," someone yelled. "Can't we all just get along?"

"Hell muthafucking nah!" one of the dudes from my school said. "Stay the fuck off our turf!"

When all was said and done, it was war with black students against the white students. Niggas didn't even know what they were fighting for, they were just swinging fists and throwing any objects they could possibly find. I spotted Romeo almost get his head busted with a steel pipe, but he ducked. It shaved his forehead, and that's when I ran over to help. We beat the shit out of that fool, leaving him lying near lifeless on the ground. It wasn't long before gunfire rang out, and just as I was scurrying to Romeo's car, a dude with a knife in his stomach fell helplessly in front of me. I jumped over him like a hurdle, and dove into the backseat of Romeo's car. He skidded from the parking lot with the back door flying open. Hearing the police sirens caused some fear to show up, but when we were out of sight, Romeo pulled over to the curb and we cracked the fuck up.

"That was some wild shit," he said, looking in the rearview mirror at the blood dripping from a cut on his forehead.

I looked at the cut. "Nigga, you all right?"

"Yeah, I'm good. Got myself another li'l soldier mark, but I'm straight."

Romeo spit on a napkin and dabbed his bloody forehead with it. Once the cut was clean, I checked the soldier mark I'd gotten on my elbow when it scraped the ground. I predicted that it wouldn't take much time to heal, and until next time, everything was everything.

Chapter 4

The police had been around asking questions about the mini race riot, but no one was snitching. The stab victim was in the hospital, and according to everyone at school, he survived. As far as I knew, no one had been arrested, and that was good news for me.

The students in Ms. Macklin's class had taken their seats. I sat at the table next to Ms. Macklin's desk, minding my own business. Nadine's face was messed up, and it surprised me how much damage I'd done. It didn't seem like I'd punched her that many times, but one side of her face was swollen and her eye was blackened. When some of the students had asked her what happened, she told them she was in a car accident. Still, some of the students didn't believe her since they had seen the entire incident go down. Ms. Macklin kept eyeballing Nadine, and during our study time, she called Nadine into the hallway. Nadine never looked my way, but I could see her through the small window talking to Ms. Macklin. Ten minutes later, they came back into the room. Nadine looked at me, and I avoided her by dropping my head. The classroom remained quiet, and when the bell rung, everyone gathered their books to leave. To no surprise, Ms. Macklin stopped me.

"Have a seat, Jamal. We need to talk."

All of the students left, and Ms. Macklin sat next to me at her desk. She gave me a look of disapproval and crossed her legs.

"I don't know where to start. But please, please tell me that you did not do that to Nadine's face."

I looked down at the table, feeling deeply ashamed for what I had done. There was no excuse for it, but at the time, I felt as if I had to defend myself. As always, I had been in survival mode, and she'd just happened to fuck with me at the wrong time. "I don't even know why I'm sittin' here talkin' to you about this, 'cause ain't no way in hell you gon' understand why somethin' like that happened. I ain't makin' no excuses, but Nadine came at me with a bat, tryin' to hurt me. I did it in self-defense."

Ms. Macklin slowly shook her head. "So, in other words, your actions were justified? You weren't man enough to walk away, or, better yet, call someone to get her away from you, huh? She was so powerful that she was going to bust your head wide open and you were going to let her. Shame on you, Jamal. Shame on you for not seeking an alternative in that situation. I am so surprised by this. You just didn't strike me as the kind of young man who would do something like that."

I felt terrible and still couldn't raise my head. "Maybe I could have handled the situation differently, but I wasn't thinkin' about how to deal with it that day. All I was doin' was protectin' myself from harm. Nadine was losin' it. She—"

"Stop it," Ms. Macklin said, pointing her finger at me. "Take responsibility for what you did, and let's see about getting you some help. There is never any excuse for putting your hands on a girl or a woman. And you—"

I raised my head. "I don't need no fuckin' help. Like I said, she tried to hurt me. You say it ain't never no excuse, but what if a stupid bitch is tryin' to kill me? If she had hit me with that bat, I could be dead right now and—"

She was blunt and cut me off. "Were you abused as a child, Jamal? Why do you feel as if what you did was okay?"

I stood up, as I definitely wasn't trying to hear this shit. "Look, I'm out of here. Do whatever you have to do, and if I get suspended for doing somethin' that was off school premises, so be it."

Ms. Macklin took my hand and held it with hers. Just the tiny touch of her hand calmed me. "I don't know what it is that you're going through, but I'm here to help you. I'm not sure how I'm going to handle this, but whatever I decide to do, just know that it will be in your best interest. I know you're a good guy, Jamal, but sometimes good people make bad decisions. You're seventeen, almost eighteen years old, and you're just a junior in high school. You still have one more year to go, but the reckless path you're on may prohibit you from graduating. Don't do this to yourself, okay?"

I was choked up inside, but would never let anyone see me cry. The truth of the matter was that I had cried, many times, because of the messed-up situation I was in. I felt sad about it, but didn't know how to find a way out. It was so damn easy for people on the outside to judge me, but nobody knew how hard it was for me to change course. Either way, I told Ms. Macklin that I would do better, and I guessed that doing better was worth a try.

My thoughts were short-lived, because as soon as I got home I found Raylo sitting his gangsta ass in the recliner, watching TV. He was chomping down on the chips, cookies, and soda I had gotten the other day from the grocery store, and to me that was a bold move. He rarely brought food into the house, and just because he bought me clothes from time to time that gave him no right to eat my food.

"Nigga, what you doin'?" I asked, snatching my bag of chips from his hand.

He jumped up from the chair, shoving me backward. His face scrunched up, and he spoke like gunpowder was trapped in his throat. "Boy, are you outta yo' rabbit-ass mind? Don't you ever take shit from me, especially after how much I contribute to this shack-ass crib."

Mama rushed into the room, closing her silky flowered nightgown to cover her naked body.

"What's goin' on in here?" she asked.

"That punk-ass son of yours snatched those chips out of my hand. You'd better get that nigga before I kill him."

Mama had the audacity to look at me and demand that I give Raylo *my* chips back. My face crumbled and steam was shooting from my ears. "Are you out of your goddamn mind? I ain't givin' him shit! What in the fuck has he ever givin' me, huh? Tell me that."

Mama placed her hand on my heaving chest, and Raylo stood with a smirk on his face. "Just give him the chips, Prince. I don't want any trouble, and I will go to the store right now to buy you some more."

"Nah, don't worry about it. You ain't never gotta do nothin' for me." To prevent her from catching a beat down tonight, I threw the bag of chips at Raylo. They flew out in his face, and many of them fell to the floor. He bent down and picked up one chip. He then put it in his mouth and smacked.

"Damn, these muthafuckas good. Being on the floor makes them taste even better. Now, I've played around with yo' ass long enough. Get the fuck out of my face befo' I crack it."

I swore I wanted to kill this dude, but I knew it would mean trouble for my mama. She pleaded for me to go to my room, but before I did, I turned to Raylo. "Don't touch nothin' else in this house that belongs to me. And if you touch my mother again, I swear to God, man, it's gon' be you and me."

Raylo sarcastically shook his whole body and chuckled. "I'm tremblin' all over, young blood. Scared as shit about what you gon' do to me. In my day, I could snap my finger and niggas like you would disappear. You'd better be thankful that I got loves for your mama, and I ain't tryin' to brang no hurt to her. You lucky, bro. All I can say is your black, stankin' ass is l-u-c-k-y."

I went to my room, slamming the door behind me. Again I wanted to cry, but instead I screamed. I picked up my football and threw it into the wall. It put a slight hole in it, then bounced back and broke my lamp. The light went out, and I sat on my bed in the darkness. Beads of sweat dripped from my forehead, and to cool myself down, I got up to turn on my fan. I sat up on the bed, and minutes later a light knock was at my door. Mama opened it, then closed the door behind her.

"Are you all right?" she asked.

"Fine," I snapped, then fell back on the bed.

"I'm sorry about what happened, and when I go out tonight I'll bring back your chips. Raylo don't mean no harm, Prince, and the two of you need to learn how to get along. He gon' be here for a while, you know what I'm sayin'? I need him to help me, and I ain't never had a man who helped me like he does. I'ma talk to him too, but in the meantime, chill out and let your mama handle this."

"You always do, Mama. No doubt, you always do."

***

Homecoming was just around the corner, and I hadn't decided yet who I would take, if anyone. Romeo and Sabrina had broken up, and not because he had hit it and moved on. He realized that she wasn't upping nothing, and it wasn't long after that he started singing bye-bye. Many of the girls at our school pretty much knew how it went down. There wasn't no need to be playing that "I'm saving myself" bullshit, especially when 80 to 90 percent of the students were already having sex. It was easy to get, and for those who weren't upping it, there were far more who would. I took those kinds of things into consideration as I tried to make a decision about who to take to homecoming. Then, it hit me: I hadn't spoken to Monesha since our encounter in Romeo's car, but all I had to do was make a few phone calls to reach her. She would be perfect. I knew the girls from our school wouldn't like it, but I needed some action as well as some fun. I made some calls that night, hooked up some shit on Facebook, and minutes later I was talking on the phone to the girl of my choice.

"Why you ain't been tryin' to get at me, ma?" I asked while sitting on the floor next to my bed.

"I have been. I told my friend, Chloe, who goes to your school, to give you my number. She said she did, but since you hadn't called, I figured you were reluctant to hook up again."

"Nah, she ain't give me nothin'. You should have known better than to do somethin' like that, especially if she got friends at my school."

"Yeah, she does. Friends who"—Monesha cleared her throat—"I heard you know very well."

I knew exactly who Monesha was talking about, but I changed the subject. "So, uh, when I'm gon' get a chance to see yo' fine self again? Girl, you got me over here thinkin' about what happened between us that night, and I'm ready for some more."

"Me too, but I thought you had made up with that girl you had a fight with that night. Chloe told me her name was Nadine and said that she was pregnant by you."

"If she pregnant, it ain't by me. Them bitch . . . girls at my school play too much. They be all up in my business, that's why I don't want to take any of them to our homecoming dance. You wanna go with me?"

Monesha didn't hesitate. "Hell yeah. I'll go, but I wish you would have told me sooner. Now, I gotta rush out to the mall to find something to wear. What colors do you want to go with?"

"Blue and black. Those are my favorite colors. I'll pick you up next weekend, and if you get a chance, why don't you come to the game?"

"Y'all gon' win this time, right?" She laughed.

"Let's just say that if we don't win, you don't have to give me none of that sweet snatch."

She laughed. "Oh, I'm gon' give you some of that. Win or lose."

I touched myself, feeling horny as ever. I couldn't wait for next weekend to come, and had already started to count down the days.

The game was a complete shutout, thirty-two to zero, and I was proud as ever. Coach Johnson was riding my nuts, and so was everyone else on the team. This time, I'd made three touchdowns, and had rushed for over one hundred yards. The scouts had already been checking me out, and Coach Johnson told me that things were starting to fall in place. I was starting to get hyped about football; after all, I had no idea where it would take me. With that being said, I hurried home to change clothes, but couldn't get dressed fast enough because the phone kept ringing.

"What is it?" I said, yelling at Romeo.

"What kind of car are you drivin'?"

"I was gon' drive my mama's Cavalier, but I'm feelin' fly tonight. Kinda thinkin' about jackin' somebody for a Chrysler 300 or somethin'."

"Sounds like a plan to me. I'm gon' cruise in the Impala, and called to see if you wanted me to pick you up, but if you gon' do it like that, go ahead and do you."

"I'm runnin' a li'l late, so I'll see you at the school."

Romeo called me a lucky dog for bringing Monesha to the dance, but his date wasn't bad either. She was a black basketball player from another school and had a pretty decent reputation. How Romeo pulled that off, I wasn't sure.

Dressed to impress in my black pants and blue silk shirt, I left the house in Mama's Cavalier. I drove around for a while, scoping cars to see who would become my next victim. This shit wasn't personal, I just needed a fucking car. I couldn't go pick up a fine-ass bitch like Monesha, who lived in the suburbs, in no jacked-up Cavalier with dents in it. As planned, I spotted a white woman parked at a stoplight, gazing into her rearview mirror. She was sliding on some lipstick, while teasing her hair at the same time. She drove a pearly white Chrysler 300 with a cream leather interior. That sucker was bad, and I had to have it. The Cavalier was already parked at McDonald's on Natural Bridge, so I rushed up to the woman's car and stuck my Glock into the lowered window.

"Get yo' ass out of the car! Now, bitch, and hurry up!"

The woman hands trembled, and she had already started busting out with tears. "Please don't hurt me," she cried.

I quickly shoved her away from the door, and got into her car. I sped off, swerving in and out of traffic until I felt the coast was clear. Getting comfortable, I kept my gloves on and adjusted the rearview mirror. I switched the radio station and cranked up some noise by T-Pain. In peace, I drove to Monesha's house to pick her up.

Monesha's house was made like a castle. From the outside, I couldn't even tell how many stories it was, but the whole damn neighborhood displayed lifestyles of the rich and/or famous. Now, more than ever, I was glad that I'd switched cars. I rang the doorbell, and Monesha's mother opened the door. She looked me over, and I could tell she wasn't happy about my neatly parted braids. Her eyes stayed glued to them, and she called for Monesha's father to come downstairs to meet me. I stood in the foyer, holding a white carnation corsage in my hand.

"Hello, young man," her father said, shaking my hand. "Why don't you come into the great room and have a seat. Monesha will be down in a minute."

I looked at my watch. "Nah, I'm good, sir. We already runnin' a li'l late, and time doesn't seem to be on our side."

Her uppity parents looked at each other, and her dad cleared his throat. "So, uh, what do you all have planned for after the dance? Monesha's curfew is one o'clock, and I expect her to be back here by then."

Just then, Monesha appeared at the top of the stairs. By the look of her, I surely wanted to tell her father about our plans. But, implying that I was going to fuck his daughter well, and she was going to suck my dick, that wasn't something I was willing to say. They had no idea how raunchy we were about to get, and Monesha's innocent smile had warmed their hearts over. We all watched as she came down the steps in an aqua-blue satin strapless dress. It fit her tiny waistline to a tee and showed off the curves in her hips and backside. Her long hair was parted down the middle, and lay against the sides of her face. She looked like a model in tall heels, and her dark skin was shiny, flawless, and smooth as ever. I rubbed the minimal hair on my mustache and straightened my tie. I felt as if I looked good, but there was no doubt that Monesha looked better.

"You look amazing," her mother said. She kissed Monesha on the cheek, and so did her dad. Her parents' politeness to each other and the family respect messed me up. I hadn't ever witnessed anything like it.

"Honey, I can't stress enough how beautiful you look. You and your mother did a spectacular job finding that dress."

Monesha smiled and awaited a compliment from me. I followed suit, telling her how magnificent she looked, and attached the carnation to her dress. Her parents took plenty of pictures, and, before we left, they rushed outside to take more pictures of us by the car. *If only they knew,* I thought, smiling my ass off with every single flash, while posing in front of the Chrysler. Monesha's dad reminded her about her curfew, and we got on our way to the dance.

No sooner had we gotten a mile away than Monesha cranked up the music and lifted her arms in the air.

"We're going to have ourselves some fun tonight," she said, snapping her fingers.

"I agree. I appreciate you comin' to my game today, ma, but I'm sorry that I didn't have much time to talk to you."

"That's okay. I let you handle your business, and you damn sure did that. I was like, 'That's my man right there.' Some of those chicks from your school started trippin', and when I turned to confront them, this teacher got all snippy with me. At first, I didn't know

who she was, 'cause she looked pretty young to me.
Then Chloe told me she was a teacher. She gon' tell me
to sit down and be quiet so she could watch the game. I
rolled my eyes at her, but she laughed it off. Then some
other girls . . ."

Monesha kept on yakking, and for a minute there I
tuned her out. I knew the teacher she was talking about
was Ms. Macklin. And the only reason she'd said anything to Monesha was because Ms. Macklin liked me. I
could feel it. Deep in my heart, I knew she did. Nah, she
wouldn't admit it, but sooner or later, time would tell.
Monesha kept going on and on, and, boy, was she driving me crazy. I couldn't believe I'd hooked up with such
a chatterbox; for me, silence was golden. I couldn't wait
to stick something in her mouth to shut her up.

What fools her parents had been. It was a pleasure
to see how much love they had for their daughter, but
she was putting on a big-ass front. After all, when I'd
left the house, Mama had sat on the couch and ain't
say shit to me. She didn't tell me how great I looked,
nor did she encourage me to have a good time. A curfew definitely wasn't set. I had never, ever had one.
I guessed that Mama felt that letting me use her car
was enough, but that's where she was sadly mistaken.
It wasn't enough, and that was why her car would be
parked at the McDonald's parking lot until later.

If you asked me, homecoming was pretty boring. It
was in our high school's gymnasium, which was crappy
as hell. Burgundy and gold streamers drooped all over,
and many helium balloons were tied on strings. Posters
that some of the students had made were on the walls,
and confetti was all over the floors. The hip-hop music
was live, though, so I guess I couldn't complain.

Most of the night, I hung with Romeo and some of the other players on our football team. The girls, though, seemed to be having a good time. It was a competition thing for them, and, to me, the winner of the night was Ms. Macklin. She looked dynamite. Her hair was pinned up, and the black bell-sleeved dress she wore guaranteed her a spot on the cover of *Glamour* magazine. All the fellas were checking her out, and Monesha had the nerve to get mad at me when she caught me looking Ms. Macklin over. That was why I started hanging with Romeo. This time around, I wasn't up for a bunch of arguing at no party. Besides, Nadine was there with her friends, so I kept my distance.

Drake's new hit was sounding off through the speakers in the gym, and many of the students started to dance. I looked for Monesha so we could. For a while I didn't see her, but I saw Coach Johnson and Ms. Macklin standing outside the double doors, looking to be in a heated conversation. She looked upset about something, and when he put his arms around her, I took a few steps back. If that weren't enough, he pecked her forehead and continued to look into her eyes as he spoke. As I continued to see what was up, I felt someone tap my shoulder.

"Are we going to dance, or are you going to keep chasing after her?" Monesha said.

I took Monesha's hand and we walked away from the door. We started to dance, but I couldn't help but think about what I'd just seen. Were Coach Johnson and Ms. Macklin fuckin'? It looked like it to me, and that explained why she was always at each and every game. *Damn,* I thought. *Coach Johnson had my woman and there wasn't shit I could do about it.*

My whole night was ruined, but I did my best to make the best of it. Monesha was doing her best to make me laugh, and when we sat down on the bleachers, she questioned me.

"Are you okay tonight? I mean, I thought you'd be happy that I was here with you, but you don't seem to be having a good time. Is there anything I can do to help lift your spirits?"

What the hell? I thought. At least I had something to look forward to for the night. I took Monesha's hand, and we snuck off to a nearby weight room. I checked to see if the door was open, but it was locked. I checked the doors to the small gym room and auditorium; those were locked as well. All I wanted was a quick blowjob, and when Monesha checked the janitor's closet, the door came open. We rushed inside, closing the door behind us. Monesha quickly unbuckled my pants, and they fell to my ankles. She stooped down low, easing some of the aching pain from my heart by giving pleasure to my manhood. My legs trembled from her touch. Since I didn't have any money for a motel, for now the damp-smelling closet had to do. I lifted Monesha's dress on the sides, exposing her mouthwatering pussy. She turned around, displaying the plumpness of her ass that I'd dreamed about for several nights. I moved her panties to the side, and started hitting it from behind. But just as I was getting my rhythm, somebody opened the door. My body froze, and my dick got limp. I pulled out of Monesha, wet dick and all. Monesha quickly stood up straight and we both stared eye to eye with Ms. Macklin.

"Both of you," she said, "get your clothes together, and meet me by the front doors." Avoiding my partially naked body, she turned her head. "Please pass me that mop so I can give it to Coach Johnson. He has a mess to clean up in the gym and I have a mess I need to clear up out here."

I reached for the mop, keeping my pants down to my ankles. By all means, I wasn't ashamed of what I had, and I was glad that Ms. Macklin had caught us in action. She was on me like white on rice, and I'd have bet any amount of money that she'd seen Monesha and me go into the closet. I handed her the mop and assured her that once we got our clothes together, we would meet her by the front doors.

"Hurry," she snapped, then closed the door.

I locked it and turned back to Monesha. "Bend that ass back over, ma. I ain't finished with you yet."

"But we gon' get in trouble," she whispered. "She told us to hurry up."

"We already in trouble. And I am going to hurry, once you turn around."

Monesha laughed and returned to her position. Ten minutes later, we left the closet. Ms. Macklin was standing by the front doors, gazing outside with no smile on her face. We walked up to her, hand in hand.

"I want the two of you out of here, right now. Jamal, I will be speaking to your mother on Monday, and Mr. King will, indeed, know about this. How dare you disrespect our school like this? And you, young lady, should be ashamed of yourself. What school do you attend?"

I could tell Monesha was scared, so I spoke up. "She don't go to school. She dropped out."

"That figures. But you are not welcome back into this school. Have a good night, and, Jamal, we will speak again on Monday."

She opened the door for us to leave, and that basically wrapped up my night. I drove Monesha home, left the stolen car on the highway, and walked back to Mama's car. I couldn't wait to see what Monday was going to bring. If Mama was going to be brought into the picture, another embarrassing moment was about to come.

Chapter 5

When Monday rolled around, my head was spinning from all of the drama in Mr. King's office. I couldn't believe Mama had even shown up, and she had the nerve to bring Raylo with her. She snapped at everything Mr. King said, and Raylo sat there, trying to portray a good father figure. I sat in my chair and didn't say nothing. Mr. King was waiting for Ms. Macklin to enter, and when she came into his office, she closed the door behind her. Mr. King told her to take a seat, and asked her to explain to Mama what she had witnessed.

"Ms. Perkins, I found Jamal in a very inappropriate situation at the homecoming dance. I asked him and his date to leave. Some of the things that he's been doing in and out of school are dangerous. Are you aware—"

Mama quickly cut her off. "Look, I know my child better than anyone. Mr. King told me that you caught him in a closet havin' sex with a girl. I don't understand what the big fuss is about. Y'all sittin up here like y'all ain't never done nothin' of the sort in high school. I know Jamal be havin' sex, and as long as it ain't with no boys, I really couldn't care less."

Ms. Macklin looked shocked at my mama's comment. She crossed her legs, and Raylo squinted to take a peek.

Mama cocked her head back and turned to Raylo. "I know you ain't up in here checkin' out another woman while in my presence. You have some damn nerve."

Raylo didn't like her tone, and I knew this was about to get ugly. "Watch your mouth, woman. Look like I know her from somewhere and I was just lookin'." He turned back to Ms. Macklin. "And what was it that you were sayin'?"

She swallowed and continued. "All I'm saying is that I think Jamal needs to see a counselor. There are some things—"

Mama cut her off again. "Woman, please. I guess next you're going to be telling me that he needs some Ritalin, too. Jamal doesn't need a counselor. All he may have ever needed was a strong foot in his ass, but I chose not to put my hands on my child. He ain't seeing no counselor, lady, and if you think that something is wrong with him because he likes to have sex in odd places, then I pity you. You must have one boring-ass life. Not you or no one else at this school is going to change a damn thing about my family. Understood?"

Ms. Macklin stood up. She looked at Mr. King and him only. "Do as you wish. I'm done with this. This explains many of my unanswered questions."

She left Mr. King's office, and Mama threw her hand back at her. Raylo checked out her backside, still insisting that he knew her from somewhere.

"If there will be nothin' else," Mama said to Mr. King, "we're leavin'. Tell me what happens to my son, and if you don't want him at this school just for having an overactive dick, then so be it."

Mr. King cleared the mucus from his throat. "There's so much more to it than just that, Ms. Perkins. You don't understand how serious this matter is. Jamal will be suspended for ten days, and during that time I do not want him on school premises. He is not allowed to play in any football games. He can check his homework online. If he doesn't have a computer at home, then I suggest he go to the library."

Mama tucked her purse underneath her arm and pursed her lips. "And this school is supposed to be helpin' kids. Tuh, right. I saw two girls pregnant when I came up in here, and these hoes around here be ringing my phone twenty-four seven. You need to be in here talkin' to their parents because these fast-tail girls are the ones around here givin' it up. My son is just takin' what's bein' offered to him, and if you think he is the *only* problem up in here, then you're dumber than I thought. The problems with this school are much bigger than him, and I hope like hell that you at least see that."

Mr. King sat silently, and we all left together. The next ten days of my life would be pure, deep hell. I would choose going to school any day over being at home with Raylo and Mama. I surely had to keep myself busy, or, if not, find something I could get into on the streets.

Actually, the next several days at home weren't too bad. I couldn't go to practice, but the coach hadn't kicked me off the team. I guess he needed me more than he'd thought. Either way, I stayed out of Raylo's way, and he stayed out of mine. Romeo didn't go to school either, and we were in my room sitting on the floor while playing video games almost all day. I was tearing him up in a boxing match between Muhammad Ali and Joe Frazier. Of course, I was Ali.

"You be cheatin'," Romeo said, dropping the controller on the floor. "Why I can't ever win?"

"'Cause you weak, nigga, that's why."

"Nah. I can't win 'cause you proficient at this shit. That's all you do at night is play these games, stay up on that phone, and talk yo' shit on Facebook. When's the last time you talked to Nadine?"

"She called me a few times, but I keep playin' her off. I don't like how she did me that day, and then to go to school and tell Ms. Macklin that I beat her ass."

"You did, didn't you?" he laughed.

I pushed Romeo's arm and stood up. "Hell, yeah. She shouldn't have come at me with no damn bat. If I didn't do that shit, these fools around here would think I'm soft. I can't let nobody think no shit like that, 'cause that fa'sho ain't how it is."

"I ain't mad at ya. You know I would have done the same thing. I asked if you spoke to her because she been runnin' around tellin' people she knocked up by you."

I threw my hand back. "I've heard it all before. Monesha asked me the same thing, and, like I told her, Nadine's baby belongs to one of them white boys. Nadine was fuckin' around with him too. Ain't no way in hell she gon' put no baby off on me."

"You know that's how they do it. You should have expected her to try some shit like that. She, of all people, was anxious to go around claimin' a baby by the almighty Prince."

We laughed again. I sat on my bed, lit a joint, and turned up the music. I took two hits from the joint, then passed it to Romeo.

"When's the last time you talked to that fly-ass Monesha? Man, she looked good enough to eat at the homecomin' dance. I would have tackled that ass in a closet too. My date, however, wasn't 'bout nothin'. We did our business in the car and I haven't spoken to her since."

"I haven't spoken to Monesha either, but I know one thing—my dick been feelin' kind of strange. It's leakin' and shit. And I got a burnin' sensation when I pee. You know I had chlamydia before, but this a different feelin'."

"What you mean by leakin'? Leakin' what?"

"Shit, I don't know," I said, standing and pulling down my navy blue sweatpants. I examined my dick, and showed Romeo the leaking I was referring to. "That shit right there."

Romeo squinted at it. He frowned. "Man, you'd better go see about that shit." He pulled his pants down and pulled out his dick. "You see this right there," he said, pointing to a scab on his shaft. "That's what healing herpes look like. You remember when I told you I got that shit last year, right? Well, that shit be comin' and goin'. It hurt like hell, too, but what you got don't look like this."

My door flew open. "Prince, turn that goddamn music . . ." Mama looked at both of us with our pants down, and dropped to her knees. "Lawd, please! Help this child of mine. He confused, and I will kill him dead in my house for havin' sex with another boy!"

Romeo and I quickly pulled up our pants, shaking our heads. "Mama, get up. It ain't like you ever told me nothin' about sex, but I was just showin' Romeo a li'l leakage problem I got. He showed me some shit he got too."

She quickly rose, wrinkling her nose. "What kind of leakage problem you got?"

I didn't want to say anything to her, but I knew she'd push me. "I think I got chlamydia, gonorrhea . . . somethin'."

Mama looked at Romeo. "You too?"

"Ms. Perkins, I got herpes, but it's under control."

Mama skeptically closed the door behind her. She turned to us, pointing her finger back and forth at the both of us. "Y'all some nasty-dick Negroes, and that's why all these women and girls around here fucked up now. Don't be usin' the bathroom in my house, Prince, and you neither, Romeo. If y'all have to go, you'd better take your asses outside." Mama looked at the lit blunt in the ashtray and walked up to it. The smoke coming from it was cooking up an addictive smell in my room, and she obviously couldn't resist. She got ready to take a hit, but laid it back on the ashtray.

"Y'all hands been on that thing. What in the hell was I thinkin'? Stop standin' there lookin' stupid and go find yourself a shirt to put on. You goin' to the health clinic right now, no ifs, ands, or buts about it."

I looked at Romeo. What the hell, I didn't have nothing to lose.

An hour later, Romeo, Mama, and I sat in chairs at the health clinic, waiting for someone to call my name. The shit was embarrassing, but funny as hell. Romeo and I couldn't stop laughing at the numerous people we saw. They looked just as embarrassed, and nobody was making eye contact. There were some fine chicks in there, too, and when my eyes finally connected with one of them, Mama smacked me on the back of my head.

"Do you got a problem?" she said loudly. "Maybe I do need to be enrollin' your butt into a sex addiction program. You need to ignore these tramps and calm your hyped tail down."

Two girls in the corner giggled and covered their mouths. Romeo laughed, but I didn't see shit funny. I moved away from Mama, and took a seat close by the exit door.

When all was said and done, I found out that this time I had gonorrhea. I got a shot, and was given some pills and a box of condoms. I was asked to contact any and all sexual partners I'd had within the last six months, and was encouraged to strap it up. Mama was yelling the same thing, and on the drive home she kept going on and on about my sexual appetite, making babies, and trifling girls.

"If you let them, they are goin' to be your downfall. I'm not takin' care of nobody's babies. If I wanted more I would have had more. You'd better use those condoms, boy. You can't ever say that I didn't warn you."

Mama was warning me, but she was five years late. I'd been fuckin' since I was twelve, and if I did use a condom, it would be a first.

Mama dropped Romeo off at home. He lived with his grandmother. His mother was in prison and his father was dead. His grandmother was the sweetest woman ever, but she had no control whatsoever over Romeo. Like me, he was just out there with little guidance, trying to make a living and doing it big as a street soldier in the Lou.

Later that day, I sat naked on my bed. It was somewhat chilly outside, but my room was hot and stuffy as hell. I didn't know what the hell was wrong with me, but I got up to crack the window a little higher. Black iron bars covered the windows, so I didn't have to worry about anyone trying to come in on me. I sat back on the bed, and covered myself with a sheet. I then picked up the phone and dialed Monesha. It had been about three weeks since I'd last spoken to her. She immediately answered.

"Hi, Prince," she excitedly said.

"Say, bitch. You fucked me up and need to take your triflin' ass to the clinic. Don't call my house no more, and, per Prince, you can take that contagious pussy of yours elsewhere."

I hung up.

Minutes later, as I was still in bed getting high, Raylo entered my room. He stood in front of my TV, blocking it so I couldn't see.

"Say, uh, you got a minute to talk, young blood?"

"Sure," I said, relieving myself of the joint.

"I've been meanin' to get at you about that teacher of yours, Ms. Macklin. I want you to see about hookin' a nigga up with her. She cold, man, and I ain't been able to keep my mind off that bitch since I seen her. That's, of course, with no offense to your mama."

No, this muthasucker didn't! Yeah, Mama had caught him cheating on her several times before, but I couldn't believe he had come into my room with this bull, expecting me to hook him up with somebody behind my mama's back. And Ms. Macklin, too?

I shook my head. "Nah, bro, that ain't gon' happen. Besides, Ms. Macklin is married," I lied. "And the last time I checked you were still with my mama, right?"

Raylo pulled out a wad of money, gripping it with his fat, ashy hand that had gold rings tightened on every finger. He licked his thumb and flipped through his dollars. "I understand your concerns, young blood, and I knew my suggestion would be a problem." He reached out to give me a hundred dollar bill and I took it. "With that being said, ain't no way in hell Ms. Macklin married. She work down there at that strip joint on the other side of town, and that's where I seen her at befo'. Married or not, though, she need to get at me."

I touched my mustache, thinking about what Raylo implied. "Nah, you got the wrong chick. Ms. Macklin ain't doin' it like that, and I know that fa'sho."

"I'm good at recognizin' people, young blood. If you wanna put some money on it, we can. In the meantime, hook a nigga up, all right?"

He flipped through a few more bills, adding $300 more to what he had already given me. I wasn't about to turn down no money, so I told Raylo that I would make sure Ms. Macklin got his number. He left my room feeling real good, and offered to take me to the strip club so I could see for myself the woman he claimed to be Ms. Macklin.

It was back to school for me, and I couldn't believe all of the drama that had happened in ten days. Last night, Romeo and I got into a knockdown, drag-and-kick-them-niggas-while-they-on-the-ground fight in our neighborhood. It was all over some chick who had been trying to get at Romeo, but her baby daddy was in a gang. My body was aching all over. I still had one fool's blood on my shoes, and before going to school I had to rinse off my Jordans.

Then, somebody had broken into Romeo's house. His grandmother was crying her heart out, only to find out that it was her thirty-one-year-old son who had stolen her shit. At first, she blamed it on Romeo, but he had never stolen a thing from his grandmother. He had her back, and she had his. We had to go confront his uncle, and, during that time, we had to shake, rattle, and roll again. His uncle was a crackhead, but that didn't stop him from talking shit. As he spoke, Romeo just busted the fool clean in his mouth. We cleaned his pockets, and found some of the jewelry he'd taken from his own mother. The flat-screen television he'd taken was broken, so we couldn't salvage that. And to top off everything, the cops had been coming around, trying to crack down on carjackers. Just the other day, I'd gotten me a Mercedes. That sucker had a tracking device in it, and after I wiped it down real good, I ditched it. I didn't have no priors, so I wasn't too worried about getting caught. It sure was nice to ride in, though, and I made a mental note to someway or somehow get me one of those suckers for myself.

In my first-hour class, Mr. Betts was working my nerves. His breath was stankin' as he hovered over me, trying to show me all of the assignments I'd missed. I expected the same routine to go down with my other classes, and I wasn't up to catching up on so much missed homework. I had planned to do what I knew best. That was, get somebody else's paper to copy and be done with it. Hell, I had already failed before, but that wasn't because I was a dummy. I just wasn't going to school and had missed sixty-one days out of the year. Missing that many days would put me another year behind. I was supposed to graduate this year, but unfortunately for me, I was already one year behind.

When I got to Ms. Macklin's class, she hadn't made it in yet. I laid a piece of paper on her desk with Raylo's phone number on it. Also, I had written a note asking if she worked at a strip club. My apologies were expressed if I was wrong, but I told her it was something Raylo wanted to know.

Before Ms. Macklin came into the room, Nadine entered. Every time she saw me, her lips were poked out and she treated me as if I didn't exist. That was so funny to me, simply because she'd been calling me. I guess she had to put a front on for the other girls, but, again, that's just how they were. As she walked by me, I whispered her name.

"What?" she snapped, then turned her head to the side to look at me.

"There's a rumor goin' around that you're pregnant. Are you sayin' it's by me?"

Her neck started to roll. I was starting to despise her more and more by the day. "It is by you and you know it. But I'm gon' handle mine and you need not worry."

I held out my hands. "Hey, ain't no sleep lost here. You need to stop lyin' on a nigga and tell the truth. Besides, I ain't even cum in you, girl. My dick can't make babies, and when that mutha come out lookin' like powder I want an apology."

Nadine started going off on me and Ms. Macklin came in. She slammed her books on her desk, causing everyone to get quiet.

"Please," she yelled. "I could hear all the loud talking down the hallway. Go have a seat Nadine, and, class, open your books to page 131."

Ms. Macklin rubbed her forehead to ease the tension. As we opened our books, I saw her reach for the note on her desk and open it. She read it, and without saying one word or looking my way, she tossed the note in the trash.

She let out a deep sigh and placed her hand on her hip. She scribbled a math equation on the chalkboard and turned to the class.

"Somebody come up here and work this," she said, holding the chalk in her hand.

Nobody moved, and everyone was looking around at each other. I looked at the algebra equation on the board again, and, knowing how to work it, I stood up. My torn jeans were low, so I pulled them up a bit to cover my drawers. Ms. Macklin handed me the chalk, and before I worked the problem, I rubbed my chin, pretending to be in deep thought. I looked at the tats on my muscular arms, and slightly lifted my body-hugging shirt to massage my tight abs.

"Let's see," I said.

Ms. Macklin sighed. "Will someone else come up to the board—"

"Hold up, ma," I said. "I got this."

"Ms. Macklin," she said with snap in her voice, correcting me. "I'm not your ma."

I begged to differ, but didn't challenge her. Instead, I worked the algebra equation and placed the chalk back on the board. Ms. Macklin looked it over, but couldn't find nothing wrong.

"Good job," she said, already writing another one. She gave the chalk to me again, and I completed that one as well.

"Well done, Jamal. Now, have a seat."

I took my seat, smiling my ass off. The girls looked impressed, but some of the fellas were hating.

"Everyone, do pages 131, 132, 133." Ms. Macklin paused and slowly flipped through the pages in her book. The class was moaning and groaning. She added two more pages, and the sighing got louder.

"I can add another page, if you'd like. There are only five to ten questions per page, and even though it seems like a lot of work, it's not. So get busy."

Everybody got busy, including me. I had so much work to catch up on, and before I knew it the bell was ringing. Ms. Macklin didn't say anything to me about the note, but as I was leaving the class, Romeo's ex, Sabrina, came up to me.

"I'm likin' how you do it, Prince. I saw your new pictures on Facebook, BlackPlanet, and MySpace. You need not be putting yourself out there like that. No wonder you got people out here anxious. Get at me soon, all right?"

Sabrina walked away, but before she did, she gave me her phone number. I shook my head at how scandalous girls could be, but whenever an opportunity presented itself, I had to take it into consideration.

As always, the lunchroom was packed. Romeo and I sat with some of the other players from the football team, and we were loud as ever. They'd lost the last game, and were mad as hell about me not being able to play in the next game. I hadn't spoken to Coach Johnson yet, but I saw him enter the cafeteria with Ms. Macklin. Again, they seemed to be involved in a heavy conversation. The way she looked at him was the way she looked at me. Even her smiles showed interest, and he was just as excited. They sat down in the far corner, eating their lunches together. I couldn't keep my eyes off of them, and that's when Romeo poked me in my side.

"What you lookin' at?" he asked.

I lowered my head and scooped my fork into the mashed potatoes. "Nothin'. Just thinkin' about some shit, that's all."

"Like what?"

"Like why in the hell your trick Sabrina been tryin' to get some of this," I said, grabbing my crotch.

Romeo cocked his head back. "What? When?"

"Today, right after Ms. Macklin's class, Sabrina gave me her phone number."

I removed the piece of paper with her number on it from my pocket and gave it to Romeo. "Okay, so she playin', right? She gon' hold back on me, but throw that shit at you? Okay, we gon' see about that shit."

"I'm gon' see about it too," I laughed.

Romeo looked shocked again. "So, are you gon' fuck her?"

"Hell yeah, I am. Why shouldn't I? She ain't with you no more."

Romeo scratched his head. "That's fucked up, Prince, but do you."

"Nigga, I know you ain't mad. If you are, then I won't hit it. Personally, I think we should run a train on that bitch. That way you can get what was already due to you."

Romeo smiled and nodded. "Yeah. Brang your condoms, bro, and a whole lot of them 'cause I ain't tryin' to get no mo' diseases. Sabrina ain't nothing but a trick, and I lost respect for her, trying to get with you."

We slapped hands together and wiggled our fingers. I got up from the table to dump my tray in the trash. I was on my way to talk to Coach Johnson, but stopped at a table full of giggly girls.

"What y'all laughin' at?" I asked.

"You," one of them said. "Is it true that you got three babies on the way? I know you ain't doin' it like that."

"I got skills, but my sperm can't make no babies. These chickenheads around here lyin' on me, and y'all need to stop believin' everything y'all hear."

Another one of the girls squeezed the muscles in my arm and observed my tats. "How you get your body like that?" she asked. "You straight, dude."

"Playin' football and liftin' weights."

"Are you playing in the game this weekend?"

"I don't know yet," I said, looking over at Coach Johnson, who was getting up from the table. I winked at the girls. "I'll be back."

Their eyes stayed glued to me as I walked up to Coach Johnson.

"Say, Coach, can we talk?"

"Sure," he said, then turned to Ms. Macklin. "I'll see you later, okay?"

She nodded and we left to go talk in his office. Coach Johnson invited me to have a seat, and he sat in the squeaky leather chair behind his overly cluttered desk.

"I was wondering if I could play in the game this weekend."

"No."

"Why not?"

"Because you haven't been to practice, and it's not fair to the team if you're allowed to play."

"I already talked to the fellas on the team and they want me to play."

"Well, they don't call the shots around here, I do. And I say no way, no how, and no can do."

"We both know that you gon' have a losin' season if you don't put me in. Why you trippin' with me, Coach? You know I wanna play."

Coach Johnson sucked his teeth and put his hands on top of his head. "We're already having a losing season, and I want to know why you keep trippin' with me," he said.

"I wouldn't exactly call losin' two games havin' a losin' season. I ain't trippin' with nobody, I'm just tellin' the truth."

"I'm being truthful with you too. You're not playing this weekend, and you won't play the following weekend unless you come to practice. The end of the semester is coming, and I hope your grades are straight. If not, I'm taking you completely off the team."

I lowered my head and rubbed my forehead. "This all about Ms. Macklin, ain't it? You trippin' with me because of her."

He immediately got defensive. "What? You'd better stop talking crazy. This has nothing to do with Ms. Macklin, and, quite frankly, if it weren't for her you would have been off the team."

"Then you're upset because your woman lookin' out for me, right?"

He chuckled. "She's not my woman. Why in the hell would you imply something like that?"

"'Cause I know she your woman just by the way she looks at you."

Coach Johnson cleared his throat and stood up. "I'm not having this conversation with you, Jamal, and if anything is going on between me and Ms. Macklin, that's our business."

"It's your wife's business too. I'm surprised that you don't wear your weddin' ring at work, but that would bring about too much trouble if you did." I stood up, looking eye to eye with Coach Johnson. "You're right, we don't need to have this conversation. Just think about what I said about wantin' to play. I'd love to play this weekend, and it would overwhelm my heart if you would reconsider."

Coach Johnson didn't say anything else to me, and my suspicions were confirmed. He was fucking Ms. Macklin behind his wife's back. As far as I was concerned, everybody had skeletons. They were all preaching to me about doing the right things, and weren't even doing the right things themselves. Technically, everyone in the school, and the school itself, disappointed me. Even Sabrina. Romeo and me pulled our train that night, and her good-girl status, through the eyes of many, had turned to ho status.

Chapter 6

I was back in the game that Coach said I wouldn't be able to play in, and after that one, we were on our way to another winning streak. Ms. Macklin seemed real uptight in class, but she need not have worried because their secret was safe with me. I wasn't thrilled about it, but, damn. She wasn't giving me no play, and Raylo was mad as hell that she hadn't called him. He wanted me to go to the strip club with him on Tuesday, in the hopes that I'd be able to hook something up. I kept telling that fool he had the wrong person, but there wasn't a chance in hell that I was going to turn down going to a strip joint. I hadn't made that kind of move yet, but Raylo told me that his friend worked the door and I'd have no problem getting in. I was all for it.

Until then, after the game that day, I went home. While lying across my bed, I thought about what I was going to do for my eighteenth birthday. It was two days before Christmas, and for many years, I'd celebrated it with Romeo. Years ago, Mama stopped acknowledging it. She said there wasn't no need, and that had gone for Christmas too. The only thing I was looking forward to was getting older and getting high. I was doing that throughout the year, but I had hoped to do something more interesting.

Tuesday had arrived, and during Ms. Macklin's class, I kept getting a visualization of her swinging on a pole and making her ass clap. I couldn't help it; my dirty li'l mind needed a serious cleaning. I tried to finish my work, but it was hard to. Besides, Nadine's belly was protruding a little. She for damn sure was pregnant. That distracted me as well, and if she was carrying my baby, there was nothing I could do about it. I didn't have a job and I really wasn't trying to be nobody's daddy. I knew I had come inside of her numerous times, but I had hopes—very high hopes—that the baby belonged to that white boy.

Romeo was talking about breaking into a house tonight, but I had other plans. According to him, his Uncle Joe, who he was selling weed for, knew a couple on the south side who had an unlocked safe in their basement. He claimed it was full of goods, but needed a couple of people to help him unload it. Any other time I was game, but I was looking forward to going to the strip club with Raylo. I told Romeo I'd catch up with him later, and I jetted home to take a nap so I could be well rested.

Around 9:00 P.M., I woke up and changed into my sagging, well-pressed jeans, black Timberlands, and an oversized black button-down cargo shirt with pockets. My braids needed to be redone, so I tied a black scarf around my head, knotting it in the back. I put on my black jacket with fur around the collar, then sprayed on a hint of cologne. Afterward, I headed to the living room to catch up with Raylo. He was ready to go, dressed like a true pimp in an orange linen suit he'd gotten from Harold Pener, and cream and orange Stacy Adams shoes. His hair was slicked back and his rugged goatee was trimmed.

"Well, well," Mama said with a shocked look on her face. "Look at the two of you. I hope this party Raylo takin' you to is legit. I don't want to hear about a bunch of foolishness between y'all."

Raylo looked at me, knowing that he had lied to Mama about where we were going. "You ready?" he said.

"Ready as I'm gon' ever be."

Raylo gave Mama a kiss and we jetted. He drove his older model gray Cadillac, which had a slight lean to it. At first, inside of the car was pretty quiet, but when Raylo and me started sharing a joint, the conversation picked up. It seemed like we were driving for a long time. He hadn't lied when he said that the strip club was on the other side of town. The roads were dark, and then, all of a sudden, lighted NAKED GIRLS signs were on display. The area got brighter and brighter, and when we finally made it there, I couldn't believe my eyes. The parking lot was packed. Trucks, RVs, motorcycles, and a whole lot of cars were everywhere. This definitely wasn't an all-black establishment, and there was no way in hell that Ms. Macklin would be found at a joint like this.

Raylo took one last hit from the blunt and sipped from a pint of Hennessy. I drank from the Hennessy bottle too, and both of us were high as hell. As soon as we got to the door, a near-300-pound white bouncer with veins popping out of his neck stopped us. He looked into Raylo's eyes and laughed.

"What's up, my nigga?" he said with a deep, strong voice, slapping Raylo's hand. "Come on in."

I wasn't feeling the white man calling Raylo a nigga, and the shit didn't sit right with me. Raylo, however, gripped my shoulder, obviously seeing my tenseness. "Young blood here with me tonight," he said. "Nigga, go find us a section in VIP."

They both laughed. Raylo and I followed the big dude. My eyes were popping out of their sockets. This was too much for a young man like me to witness, but

I wasn't complaining. My only complaint was the smell of wild ass, covered with sweet perfumes. Pussy was everywhere, though. Half-naked ladies were sashaying around, rubbing their bodies against men and women. The music was thumping loudly and the place was clouded with thick white smoke. White, blue, and yellow lights were spinning everywhere, and plenty of disco balls were turning. The bouncer sat Raylo and me in a purple leather circular booth that had lit candles all around to light up the area. Some of the other older men he knew were there, and Raylo continued to introduce me as his li'l nigga. I wished like hell that Romeo could have come with me. There was no way he would believe what my eyes were, indeed, witnessing.

I could barely sit down before a Latina chick came into the VIP section, clapping her ass. She was working it hard, and the men were not only making it rain, hell, they were making it thunder! Money was being thrown everywhere, pouring down on her as she performed. I wanted to jump up and take some of that shit, but the Latina dancer's performance was worth every penny. I sat there, speechless. My mouth was wide open and I was starting to drool. Raylo came over to me, and the Latina dancer followed. She was rubbing her ass against me, and I couldn't believe when she sat on the table and pulled her g-string aside so I could see her hairless slit. Man did that shit look good. Raylo slapped his hand against my back, and he and his friends were laughing their asses off.

"What you know 'bout that, young blood? You don't know shit about that, nigga!" Obviously, I didn't. The dancer started grinding on the table, rolling herself around and sticking her fingers inside of her coochie. I couldn't believe when Raylo rubbed his finger against her stuff, and the more money he dropped on the table, the more aggressive she got. He smacked her ass, telling her to move on. She did, and he fell back on the booth next to me.

"Man, man, man!" he yelled. "Why you sittin' there lookin' lost? I thought you were into this kind of shit."

"I . . . I am, but, damn! I didn't know females be doin' it like that."

Raylo handed me a stack of ones. There had to be at least two or three hundred dollars. "Relax and enjoy yourself. Get you somethin' else to drink, and when another one of them bitches come over here, drop somethin' heavy on 'em."

He slapped my back again, and walked away to talk with some of his friends. I slowly removed my jacket, still mesmerized by my surroundings. My eyes scanned the place. I had never in my life seen so many men with pure lust in their eyes. I was sure many of them were married, but they damn sure were there to have a good time. There was a long bar that stretched from one end of the club to the other. It was lit up with pink and white neon lights. Many rows of alcohol were behind it, and the glass mirrors viewed a spacious, marble-topped black dance floor, glistening as if it were covered in diamonds. The floor was surrounded with rails, but the floor was so big that no matter where you sat in the club, you could see the dancers. On the same floor were two circular staircases that led to the upper level. Two more dancers were on those, and, at the moment, a white chick with long black hair was doing her thing on the main floor. She was quite impressive, and I swore I ain't never seen a white chick with an ass so big.

"There go one of them whooties right there. That's what we call them white gals with big asses," Raylo said, turning to talk to me. "Lawd have mercy, would you look at that fat tail. I bet she got a gash that won't quit."

He didn't have to worry, because I was looking. I kept scanning the club, just in case I happened to see Ms. Macklin. Instead of seeing her, I did see someone I knew. I squinted, just to be sure. Directly across from us, but on the far side of the club, was my sperm donor. I couldn't believe it! I had seen that fool on the streets, many times, but he rarely said anything to me. It didn't bother me at all, simply because I hated his ass. I'd just seen him about two weeks ago, coming out of a liquor store on Goodfellow Boulevard. Mama made it clear that I was to never go anywhere near him. She also told me never to ask him for one dime. He'd been slinging dope for a long time, and everyone pretty much knew that his paper was stacked. Besides that, we looked a lot alike. He couldn't deny me, even if he wanted to. Then again, yes, he could. I watched him from afar, dropping money as if it were going out of style. That money could have been given to Mama for child support, or, for that matter, what if I wanted to take my ass to college? He was sad, and I couldn't believe that my blood was starting to boil just by looking at him. I couldn't help it; that's the kind of effect he had on me whenever I saw him.

I got up from the table and told Raylo that I was going to the bathroom. I purposely walked to the other side, just so my old dude could see me. His eyes turned in my direction, and he couldn't help but take a double look. I stared at him with a blank expression, then cut my eyes and went into the bathroom. I took a quick leak, and to my surprise, when I came out of the bathroom stall he walked in. Two of his bodyguards stood by the door, and he passed one of them his cane. I stood by the sink, washing my hands.

"Don't I know you from somewhere?" he asked.

I didn't even look at him. "Nah, I don't think so."

"You a li'l young to be chillin' in a place like this, ain't you?"

I shook the water from my hands and looked at him through the mirror. "Maybe." I shrugged. "But, you see, my mama don't give a damn if I come to places like this, and neither does my daddy. I'm pretty much doin' my own thing, simply because nobody gives a fuck."

I walked around him, making my way to the door. His bodyguards blocked me from exiting. I refused to turn around.

"It's a damn shame how your mama raisin' you. You tell that bitch I said so, and as for your father, well, you may wanna pat that nigga on his back for your good looks."

It took everything I had not to turn around and mess that fool up. I wished like hell that I had my Glock on me. If so, I would have shot him dead. His bodyguards moved aside and I left the bathroom. All kinds of bad feelings were going through me, and as interested as I was in seeing the women dance, a part of me was ready to go. Being in the same place as him wasn't a good feeling.

When I got back to the booth, Raylo and his friends had taken their seats. They were grubbing on some hot wings, and more drinks were on the table along with three slender rows of crystal white cocaine. I could see the white powder on Raylo's nose, and he invited me to take a seat next to him. I did, and he slid the cut mirror with a sliver of cocaine on it over to me.

"That there will clear your mind and relax the hell out of you. G'on and try it."

I looked across the way at my old dude, and he was certainly looking in my direction. I let off a soft snicker, then dropped my head low and sniffed hard. At first, my nose burned, then it felt like I had a brain freeze.

I wiggled my nose with my finger and closed my eyes, taking in the rush. Raylo was squeezing the back of my neck, massaging it as I cocked it from side to side. I felt very lightheaded, and my vision was starting to blur. After a while, all I could hear was loud noise. I was slumped down in the booth, and could barely see out of my lowered eyelids. With his fur coat draped over his shoulders, I noticed my sperm donor and his partnas coming our way.

Raylo shifted around in his seat, and that's when I noticed the Glock .22 by his side. My old dude stood in front of our booth and reached out his hand. Raylo slapped it with his.

"Well if it ain't Derrick low-down, dirty-ass Jackson," Raylo said. "What up, man?"

"Nothin' much. Just wonderin' why you got this young nigga up in a joint like this, that's all."

I sat up straight, and as I was about to speak, Raylo placed his hand on my chest. "I got this," he said, gazing at Derrick. "Why the fuck are you worried about who I brang up in this muthafucka? You need to get the hell out of our view, 'cause we ain't come up in here to be lookin' at no chickenhead fool who don't have the guts to take care of his own kid, let alone his son. Now, since I've been pickin' up the pieces for you, nigga, I suggest when you see me, the only thing you do is bow down to me. 'Nuff said, enough done. Get yo' pretty-boy ass out of my space befo' I bust a cap in ya."

Raylo's crew wasn't nothing to mess around with. These were some old-school gangstas, and every last one of them was strapped. Derrick was gangsta too, but obviously he knew who not to mess with. He eyeballed Raylo and cracked a smile.

"Tell Shante I said what's up." He took one last look at me and strolled away. That was fine by me, and, truthfully, Raylo was the only man I'd really known as a half-ass father. Derrick left Mama when she was pregnant, and marriage was never an option. I had no memories of his ass ever being there for me, so what Mama told me about him, I believed her.

After Derrick left, I had a burst of energy. My eyes were wide open and my heart was pumping fast. More dancers came by, but none of them looked like, or could even be compared to, Ms. Macklin. One after another, the DJ continued to announce, "Ladies and gentlemen, I bring you Destiny, Dynasty, Peaches, and Pearls." Fat Cat to Lady Ice. Raylo was hyped, and he kept telling me Ms. Macklin was coming.

As soon as he said that, he looked at the stage, claiming that she was there. When I looked, it for damn sure wasn't Ms. Macklin, but it was a black dancer who was hooked up like she was.

"Man, that ain't her," I said. "I told you you had the wrong chick, and you need to give me the hundred dollars we bet."

Raylo looked at the dance floor again, then leaned over to get his wallet from his pocket. He gave the money to me, then let out a deep sigh.

"Listen. I appreciate you comin' with me tonight, especially since you know what's up with me and yo' mama. Believe it or not, I loves yo' mama, but a woman needs to know her place. She oversteps her boundaries sometimes and that shit don't sit right with me. I ain't ever wanted to disrespect you by hittin' on her, but a man gets tired of the bullshit sometimes. As you grow up, you'll see what I mean. You gotta be in charge of yo' shit. These women out here will use what they got to fuck a nigga up. If they start wantin' to play the love game, move out. Young man like you don't need to be lovin' nobody but yourself. What I'm sayin' is don't grow up bein' like yo' damn daddy. If you got some kids, take care of them muthafuckas. I don't care how many you have, take care of 'em. Them bitches, though, let them fend for themselves. Ain't a woman up in here can replace yo' mama, and even though she's the only woman I ever loved, a player like me still likes to have his fun."

Raylo winked, and I could tell that he was beyond messed up. Then again, so was I. I'd heard what he'd said though. And even though I understood what he was saying about women, I didn't like the fact that he had been abusing my mama.

"I hear you, Raylo, but do me a big-ass favor."

"What's that?"

"Keep your hands off my mama. That's some shit that I can't handle, and if you can do that for me, you and me all good."

Raylo shot the glass of Hennessy to the back of his throat and cleared the burn. He nodded and massaged the back of my neck. "You got it," he said. "Never again."

We got ready to go, and just as I was putting on my jacket, Raylo started laughing and slapping my back. His eyes were focused on the dance floor.

"Boy, didn't I tell you! Give me my damn money back! Now!"

I looked at the dance floor and almost fell back in my seat. I wasn't sure if my eyes were playing tricks on me; after all, I was tremendously fucked up. The dancer on the floor sure in the hell looked like Ms. Macklin, with extensions in her hair. Her long hair was down her back, and she wore a satin silver g-string and bikini top. Black tassels hung from her nipples, and her strapped black heels were tied up to her knees. I was in complete awe. She looked even better on the floor than she did at school. Realizing that it was her, I did drop back to my seat. Raylo and his friends were playfully fanning me.

"I told you!" Raylo kept yelling while pushing my shoulder. "You'd better get up out of that seat and hook a nigga up!"

After seeing Ms. Macklin, I was trying to hook myself up. Her performance was shocking. I'd had no idea she could shake that ass like she was. She was out of control, and was doing it to Mystical's "Shake Ya Ass": "Watch yourself . . . show me what u workin with . . ." Then again, from day one I'd visualized her working over a pole. I knew there was something about the way she strutted and walked as if she was on the tips of her toes. *I'll be damned,* I thought with my eyes glued to her. She entertained the crowd, and I couldn't wait until she made her way to the upper VIP section where we were. No doubt she was coming, and the men in our section already had bills all over the place. They were making it rain, big time! And we were like a bunch of kids in a candy store, waiting to be served. I sat back at the booth, relaxing with my jacket on and the hood with fur pulled over my head. I observed her coming up the circular staircase, and, finally, making her way over to us. Her back faced me, and Raylo and his partnas were touching every part of her body that they could. A bouncer was close by, making sure that no one went overboard. My eyes scanned the flowing hair on her back, then went down to the small of her bare, sweaty back. Her heart-shaped ass had a g-string on it, but that was it. My heart was pumping faster, and when she turned around, my eyes dropped between her legs that displayed a tiny gap. The sight was too much for me to handle, and that's when I looked up and my eyes stared right into hers, causing an electrical shock for both of us. Neither of us blinked, and it was as if we were frozen in time. Her grinding hips slowed and she quickly closed her widely separated legs. I continued to look into her eyes, and when I licked my tongue across my bottom lip, she blinked. She turned around and quickly danced her way out of the VIP area.

I had witnessed it with my own eyes. Ms. Macklin was a freak! She was pretending to be something that she wasn't, and I always knew there was something up with her. Raylo couldn't stop talking about her to his friends, and, like me, they watched as she made the rest of her rounds. She wasn't shaking it like she was before, and when the music stopped, she disappeared. Ten minutes later, Raylo said that he was ready to go. I told him that I would tell Ms. Macklin about him again, and I couldn't wait to get to school tomorrow so I could see her reaction. Tonight, though, I felt as if I had turned into a man. Raylo was now my idol, and along with what he'd said, this place had me looking at girls and women a li'l differently. I'd lost even more respect, but had gained respect for the man who was starting to teach me so much.

Chapter 7

The next day things went terribly wrong. I hadn't spoken to Romeo at all, and I continued to try to get in touch with him throughout the night. I had planned to go with him to burglarize those people's house, but going to the strip club with Raylo was my choice.

During my first-hour class, the police came to my school looking for me. They hauled me down to the police station, and there I was, sitting at a table being interrogated like a brotha on *The First 48*. According to the detectives, they were looking for Romeo. Last night, he was involved in a robbery, and the white couple who owned the house was murdered. I knew Romeo well. There was no way he had killed anybody. Now, he'd kick ass in a minute. He'd stomp a nigga to the ground with no regrets. He'd blacken a bitch's eye and think nothing of it. He'd rob a person blind, but, like me, murder wasn't possible.

I sat with my head on the table and my arm stretched out underneath it. I was still tired from last night, and it was difficult listening to these fools trying to convince me that I was with Romeo last night and that I knew what had happened.

I scratched the part between my sweaty braids. My hands were wet because I was nervous, because the detectives didn't believe me.

"I swear to God that after he left my house last night I ain't seen him."

"What time did he leave your house again?"

"Around midnight," I lied. "He was at my house for most of the night, so I don't see how he could have been on that scene at nine o'clock."

"Where is he then?"

I shrugged. "I don't know. But I do know that he ain't killed nobody."

The detectives had nothing and they knew it. They kept questioning me, but I really and truly had nothing to tell. There wasn't a chance in hell that I would tell them anything about Romeo, but I was dying to find out what in the hell had actually happened.

After several more hours of interrogation, they let me go. It was too late to go back to school, and, for now, I wasn't even thinking about it. I wanted to find Romeo to see what was up. I stopped at his grandmother's house, but she too said that she hadn't seen him. She didn't seem too worried, because Romeo was known for not coming home some nights. I kissed his grandmother on the cheek and left.

At home, Mama and Raylo weren't there. I went into my room and lay across my bed. I was worried like hell, but it wasn't long before I fell asleep.

The blaring ring of the phone awakened me. When I cracked my eyes, my room was dark, and I scrambled around to find the phone. I picked it up, and, thank God, it was Romeo.

"Say, man, meet me under the bridge," he said, then hung up.

I jumped up from my bed, and it didn't take long for me to catch the MetroLink to meet Romeo downtown under the MLK Bridge. We'd hung out there a lot when we were kids, and it was sort of like our meeting place. As soon as I got off the MetroLink, I tossed my hoodie over my head to shield the blistering cold wind from blowing in my face. My hands were in my pockets as I walked abruptly down the street to get to Romeo, who I could already see. Normally, he had a big-ass grin on his face, but today things weren't looking so good. I stepped up to him, holding my hand out for him to slap it.

"What's going on, man?" I asked.

Romeo took another puff from his cigarette, then tossed it to the ground and smashed it with his shoe.

"I'm in a lot of trouble," he said. "I don't even know where to start."

Since it was so cold outside, we started walking to a nearby Greyhound bus station. It was somewhat crowded, but we sat far away from people so no one would hear us.

Romeo rubbed his hair back to wipe the sweat from his hands. I had never seen him so nervous, and when he started to tell me what had happened, I knew why.

"My uncle asked two more dudes to go to that house with us, and I didn't even know them cats. They were throwin' shit around, makin' all kinds of noises, and I told them fools to chill. We started arguin' and shit, then the next thing I knew, we heard the people come into the house. We all panicked, and instead of gettin' the hell out of there, that fool, Jake, went upstairs to confront the couple. He told me and that other cat to get the shit from the basement, and while we were downstairs, we heard a gun go off. I dropped that shit so fast, and when I got upstairs, he had put two in both of those people's heads. I don't know why he did that shit, and before I knew it, I started hearing sirens. I jumped out of a window and ran as fast as I could down an alley. Jake and that other fool broke off in another direction, but I think that other dude got caught. No doubt, that nigga been snitchin'."

I shook my head. "That's fucked up. He may have gotten caught and snitched on you, too. The police came to school today lookin' for me and you. They assumed that I was with you, but when they took me to the police station, I told them you were with me until midnight. You should tell them the same thing, and tell them that that fool lyin' on you to protect himself."

Romeo rubbed his hands together and leaned forward. "I don't know what I'm goin' to do. I really need to get the hell out of here, 'cause I got a feelin' that I'm goin' down for this shit."

"If you leave, where you gon' go? You know I'll go with you. The last thing I want is to see yo' ass behind bars."

Romeo nodded, and, for the first time, I saw the fear in his eyes. A part of me was so glad that I hadn't gone with him last night, but it still felt as if I was going through the same pain with my friend.

Romeo stood up and stretched. "As far as I can see, I'm on the run. I can't go home, I can't go to your house, and I definitely ain't takin' no chances. I'm gon' let things settle, then I'll get at you to let you know where I'm at."

"Hell, nah, nigga. Look, I'm with you on this shit. Wherever you goin', I'm goin'. I ain't got nothin' to lose, and, like always, we in this shit together. Nigga, we street soldiers. So stop talkin' that shit, and let's decide what the fuck we gon' do and where we gon' go."

Romeo cracked a tiny smile, gripping my hand again. As I stood to playfully shove his shoulder, I looked over it and saw five police officers. I couldn't get one word out of my mouth before they swarmed in on us with guns, yelling, "Put up your hands and get on the ground! Now!"

I knew that I was fast like a lightening bolt, but there was no way in hell I could outrun them. The officers snatched us up so quickly, slamming us both to the ground. Always being aggressive, both Romeo and I resisted by swinging punches to keep them away. That caused a complete scene to be made, as the officers did their best to restrain us.

"Calm down, you stupid muthafucka," one said with hatred in his eyes as he lit my stomach up with powerful punches. I doubled over in pain as I noticed the smirk on his face. Another officer punched me in my jaw. It stung like hell! I could feel the billy clubs hitting my legs and they started to buckle. I had a burning feeling in my legs and started to feel numb all over. My body felt limp, and if I even wanted to yell, "Help," I couldn't do it with an already swollen lip. The numerous people at the bus station just looked on, with no one saying one word as we were called "dumb niggers" over and over again. I glanced over at Romeo and saw that the beat down he was taking was just as intense as mine.

"It's time to get all of you damn fools off the streets. Stand the hell up and keep still." I slowly stood up with my hands cuffed behind me. Romeo did the same. Again, this shit was too embarrassing, and as everyone looked on, all they could do was shake their heads. At least one man had the courage to say something.

"All of that was unnecessary," he said to one of the cocky officers as we passed by him. "Don't be surprised if you see yourselves on the news."

He held up his phone, just so the officers could see it. All one of the officers said was, "Go to hell." He warned the man about interfering, and threatened to arrest him. This was messed up, no ifs, ands, or buts about it.

***

I had been in jail for almost twenty hours, battered and bruised and feeling like shit. I had no idea where Romeo was and that, in itself, worried me. I wanted out of this cell, and even though my springy mattress at home wasn't the best, I was dying to be on it. I figured Mama was wondering where I was; then again, she probably wasn't. There were days that I too hadn't come home, and I was sure she thought I was over Romeo's house or somewhere else chillin'. Not this time.

Almost an hour later they let me go, because they had nothing on me. I felt good about getting out of there, and as soon as I left the building, I looked around for Romeo. Maybe he had been released too. I surely hoped so, but when I didn't see him, I walked to the nearest MetroLink station so I could go home.

It was a little after 7:00 P.M., and when I walked into the house, I could hear my mama moaning and groaning about how good the dick was feeling to her.

"Fuck it, big daddy," she shouted. "Beat this pussy and keep givin' it to me."

The bed was slamming against the wall, possibly causing some cracks. I knocked on her door, just to calm the noise and let her know I was home.

"Who is it?" she yelled.

"I just wanted to let you know that I'm home."

"Uh-huh. Now, get away from my door and go somewhere and sit down."

I walked away from the door, shaking my head. I swore I hated her, but, then again, she was my mama. I went into the bathroom and looked at my face. Underneath my eye was a small bruise, and there was a cut inside of my lip. I'd gotten myself some more soldier marks. It wasn't like I hadn't had them before. When I removed my sweatpants, I noticed that bruises were up and down my legs. Those billy clubs tore me up, and, after looking at my legs, I hated the police even more. Like the man at the bus station had said, all of that was unnecessary, and I shouldn't have ever given them a reason to do this kind of shit to me. I'd seen the smirks on their faces, I could see the enjoyment in their eyes, and their racial slurs made me angry. Romeo and I were treated like we were nobody, and I didn't like that feeling at all.

I took a lengthy shower, trying to wash off the grime I'd felt from sleeping on a cot. My braids were out of whack, so I took them down and washed my hair. Afterward, I went to my room and closed the door to silence the noise Mama was still making in the bed with Raylo. My hair stood all over my head, so I got my clippers and started to shave it off. I trimmed it down, giving myself a fade and sharp lining to the best of my ability. My fade looked decent, and I had a clean-cut look that I was more than impressed with. For a second, I thought about how Ms. Macklin would like it, but at that moment, I wasn't even sure if I was going back to school. Yet again, I had missed a lot of days, and was so far behind. I had to get papers from the students in my class so I could copy them and somehow catch up. That, in itself, seemed like a lot of work, and I wasn't sure if I was up to doing it.

Waiting for Romeo to call, I lay across the bed, reading a book. During my really rough days, I always pulled out a book to read, as it helped clear my mind. It helped with my vocabulary too, and whenever I would come across a word that I didn't know, I'd reach for my dictionary. As I was looking for the definition of the word "disheveled," the phone rang. I closed the dictionary and picked up the phone next to me. I thought it was Romeo, but it was Nadine.

"Don't hang up," she said, hearing me sigh.

"What do you want, ma?"

"I was just concerned about you. The police came and got you, and nobody heard from you since."

"I'm good. But why are you worried about me?"

Nadine hesitated to answer, then spoke out. "Prince, whether you want to accept it or not, this is your baby I'm carrying. I would like you to be a part of his or her life, and it hurts me so bad that you're playing me off. I thought you cared for me, and I never would have given myself to you if I thought you'd do me like this."

It was the wrong time, and I really didn't want to hear this shit. "Didn't you have sex with that white boy?"

"No, I didn't. I don't know why you keep saying that. Just because I danced with somebody it doesn't mean I had sex with him."

"Girl, please. He was touching on your booty like he'd touched it before. Don't be lyin' to me. I know how bad you wanted to have a baby by me, and just like them other girls—"

"Do you think I planned this?" Her voice got loud and cracked. "Prince, you have no idea how much I'm dealing with right now. I haven't even told my mother about the baby, and I cry every single day because I don't know how I'm going to take care of this baby. I'll probably have to drop out of school. This is not how I intended my life to be. This is our baby, and I need your help taking care of it."

"I don't know what I can do to help you. I *still* don't believe it's mine, and I ain't ever got another girl pregnant. Why all of a sudden you are?"

"'Cause you had sex with me five times without using a condom, that's why. And from what I heard, you do have another girl pregnant. That bitch from the other school is, and I guess you're denying that baby too."

She had to have been talking about Monesha, and, as trifling as she was, I knew she wasn't putting her baby off on me. Now, I was even more frustrated. "Nadine, don't call me about this shit no more. Do what you gotta do. My suggestion to you would be to have an abortion. I ain't tryin' to be no daddy; there ain't no room in my life for that kind of shit. Tell your mother you're pregnant. You and her need to see what's up."

I hung up, and a minute later the phone rang again. I thought it was Nadine calling back, but surprisingly it was Raylo.

"Where yo' mama at?" he asked.

I wanted to say, "In her room fucking you," but obviously there was another man in there with Mama. I looked at my door with a tied tongue. "Uh, she's in the bathroom. I'll tell her to call you right back."

"I'm almost there. I changed my mind about that trip. Just wanted to see if she wanted somethin' to drink before I got there."

I got off my bed, knowing that Raylo would kill Mama if he came in this house and caught her with someone else. "Uh, yeah. Stop and get her some wine coolers. You can pick up me some too, that's if you don't mind."

Raylo chuckled and hung up the phone.

I rushed out of my room, and since the noise had ceased, I opened Mama's bedroom door without knocking. I should have known better, because she was known for getting her freak on behind Raylo's back. What did I break open the door for? She was kneeled on the floor, sucking the dick of a man I'd never seen before.

"Raylo on his way here," I said, closing the door. I could hear the scrambling going on, and I sat in the living room by the door, looking outside. I hoped that the coast would be clear before Raylo came, but that didn't happen. He pulled in the driveway and got out of the car empty handed. I guessed he hadn't stopped at the store. I noticed him look at the car parked in front of our house, and just as he came through the front door, Mama and the other dude were walking out of her bedroom. Their steps halted when they saw Raylo.

"Hey, baby," Mama said, putting on a fake grin. Raylo had a blank expression on his face as he looked at Mama, then the dude behind her.

"Who is this muthafucker?" Raylo asked.

Mama fidgeted, combing her fingers through her messy hair. "Aw, baby, this is my cousin all the way from Mississippi, Tony. Tony this is my fiancé, Raylo."

Suspicions were written all over "Tony's" face. Raylo, however, was far from being a fool. He walked past the both of them, and looked into Mama's room. The smell gave everything away, as well as the disheveled bed. There was no denying that Mama had been fucking.

Raylo's fist tightened and he reached out to grab Mama's throat. His grip was so tight that when he lifted her, her feet dangled off the floor. Tony's ol' punk ass had broke out running. Nothing but wind followed him, and the screen door slammed on his way out.

"You see what I'm talkin' about?" Raylo said loudly, looking over at me. "I try to do right by this bitch, but she keep on playin' these muthafuckin' games."

He shoved Mama backward and she fell to the ground. She crawled backward and the tears started to flow. "Raylo, I . . . I'm sorry, baby. We were just playin' around and I thought you were on your way out of town to—"

Raylo's size-fourteen shoe went right into her side as he kicked her. Mama crouched down, grabbing her stomach. That's when I stood up. I always said that I wouldn't interfere again, but I couldn't sit there and do nothing. Raylo had the look of a killer in his eyes, and as far as I could see, Mama was on her deathbed.

Raylo kicked her again, and I pushed him away from her.

"Stop, man," I pleaded. "Fuck her. You told me you wouldn't do this shit again and I took your word for it."

He gritted his teeth and pointed his finger at me. "But I also told you about these slick-ass bitches, didn't I?"

I nodded, and watched as Mama scrambled off the floor. "Help me, baby," she said to me. "Don't let him put his hands on me."

Damn, I was confused. Now, all of a sudden, she wanted my help. Minutes ago it was "get the fuck away from my door and go sit down." I wasn't about to get stabbed again by one of her boyfriends, and what Raylo said had made sense. Nadine was just like Mama, and knowing that she was lying about fucking that white boy, I reached for my jacket to go.

"Take it easy on her. And when I come back, I expect to see my so-called mama alive."

Raylo sucked his teeth, and as much as it hurt me, I walked out the door. Mama had brought that shit on herself, but I considered her a soldier, too. Like always, she'd bounce back, right back into his arms. If that was what she wanted her life to be about, so be it. I had too much on my mind to be worried about her. In situations like this one, I forced it out of my mind, but hoped it wouldn't happen again.

Chapter 8

The weekend had passed and I still hadn't heard from Romeo. I figured he was still locked up, because I knew if he was out he would have called me. I felt lost without my partna, but instead of sitting around the house, I went to school. I hadn't been in four days, and wasn't looking forward to playing catch-up. Mama had locked herself up in her room, and when she came out last night to get some water in the kitchen, I saw her bruised face. All I kept thinking was that I hoped the dick she had was good and worth it. She was alive, and should have been damn glad about that. As for Raylo, he had been nowhere around. I wasn't sure what she was going to do without him; then again, I wasn't sure how long their breakup would last. Not long, I suspected.

As soon as I got to school, everybody was questioning me, trying to find out what had happened. According to them, Romeo's picture had been on the news and he'd been arrested for the murder of a politician and his wife. Apparently, the news showed pictures of the other two men as well, and everyone was concerned about Romeo getting himself involved in so much mess. I kept professing his innocence, but that didn't do much good. People were already passing judgment, and even through the students' eyes at our school, Romeo looked guilty.

I hit up several students for their papers, and I sat in first hour trying to play catch-up. Luckily, we had a substitute teacher in Mr. Betts's class, and all she was doing was reading a magazine. I got a lot of my papers done, and at the end of the hour, I turned in my assignments for that class.

I hadn't seen Ms. Macklin since that night I'd seen her at the strip club. I was so sure I'd be looking at her in a different way, and as soon as she came in her classroom, all I could think about was her scantly dressed in that silver bikini. She seemed surprised to see me, and blinked to look away.

"Good morning, everyone," she said, putting her books on the desk. "Raise your hand if you finished your homework from yesterday."

Half of the class raised their hands. She told those students to turn in their papers, and gave them free time for the rest of the hour. The rest of us were told to complete the assignment. That gave me time to catch up on her assignments as well, but since I was copying from other people's papers, I was careful so she wouldn't see me.

Throughout the hour, I kept looking up, and Ms. Macklin was watching me. I guess she figured I would say something to her, but at this point, there wasn't nothing to say. She was a freak, putting on one hell of a front.

Ten minutes before the bell, Ms. Macklin slid a folded piece of paper underneath my book and asked me not to read it until later. I nodded and she walked away from me. When the bell rang, I quickly left, anxious to see what was on the note. I rushed to my locker, and when I opened the piece of paper I read, THIS IS MY ADDRESS. PLEASE STOP BY AROUND SIX OR SEVEN. WE NEED TO TALK.

I put the paper with her address on it in my pocket. I couldn't wait to see what she had to say for herself.

That evening, I caught the MetroLink to Ms. Macklin's ground-level apartment near downtown St. Louis. It was connected with several more apartments, and the area was quiet and kept clean. I stood on the steps with my hands in my pockets, taking deep breaths. As much as I'd always dreamed of coming to her place, I had in no way expected for it to be under these circumstances. I rang the doorbell, then heard a dog barking. Ms. Macklin told the dog to shush, and when she opened the door, she had a Chihuahua in her hand.

"Come in, Jamal," she said, rubbing her dog. "Be quiet, Haley, now shush."

The dog calmed down and Ms. Macklin put her down. She waddled away, over to her food.

"Thank you for coming," Ms. Macklin said. She was dressed in a pair of jeans and a plain blue T-shirt. She still looked sexy, even without a drop of makeup on. I followed her to the living room, where she sat back on the couch, folding one of her legs underneath her. I took a seat on the other end of the couch.

"What's up, ma? Why did you invite me over here?" I asked.

She took a moment to bite her nails. "I'm sure you know why. But first I want to ask you, how is Romeo? I know there's a lot going on, and I truly hope that you didn't have anything to do with it."

"No, I didn't. I just happened to be at a strip club that night, enjoyin' the hell out of myself. If anyone can vouch for me that night, I'm sure you can. As for Romeo, he told me that he was innocent. I believe him. My partna ain't capable of committin' no murder."

"I hope not but I'm not going to sugarcoat this for you, Jamal. From what I heard, and from what I've been hearing on the news, things don't look good for him. The people who were murdered were well known and I don't have to tell you that they were white. Romeo is going to have a difficult time defending himself, and I'm sure that he doesn't have money to pay a lawyer, does he?"

I lowered my head, thinking about all that Romeo was probably going through. I could almost feel what he was, and just from the look in his eyes at the bus station that day, I knew he was scared. "He don't have any money, and I know his grandmother ain't got it. I haven't even talked to her yet, and she probably upset with me, thinkin' I was involved too."

"Again, it's a good thing that you weren't. If or whenever you talk to Romeo, let him know that he's in my prayers. If there's anything I can do on his behalf, let me know."

I turned my head to look at her. "Like what? What can you do to help him?"

"Write a letter on his behalf, something. It may not be much, but maybe a letter from me will let the court know what kind of young man he really is. As I said, I just hate that he got involved with something like that. He really should have known better."

I sat thinking about all of the shit Romeo and I had done. It never dawned on me that we'd get caught up, especially in nothing as severe as murder. *Damn,* I thought, *this is so messed up.* Ms. Macklin watched me in deep thought, then she cleared her throat.

"I want to apologize to you for what you saw the other day. Aside from teaching, I took on an extra job to help with paying my bills. It's hard out here, Jamal. Even though many people may not approve of or understand what I do, still, it works for me. I have an ill mother I'm trying to take care of in a nursing home, and the kind of money I make helps me take care of her. There are so many things . . ."

I listened to Ms. Macklin trying to explain her situation, but she didn't owe me no explanation. It was even hard out here for a seventeen-year-old like me, and when you come from where I come from, why fantasize about shit you may, or may not, ever have? I got sick and tired of folks trying to tell me there was a way out of this kind of life. They expect people like me and Ms. Macklin to get our acts together, and when it came to young black men, they were always throwing up our black president. That was fine and dandy, but we ain't making no presidents in my hood. My idols— Nino Brown and Tony Montana—those were the kinds of men who ran through here. Ain't nothing fictional about their characters; I knew plenty of cats like them. If anything, we all had to face reality. The reality of my situation was that this was how my life was going to be, so I'd better get used to it.

"Look," I said to Ms. Macklin. "You don't owe me an explanation, and you gotta keep on doing you. If strippin' is what you gotta do, then why you sittin' here explainin' yourself to me? Honestly, I think it's kind of dope, and you damn sure have perfected your skills."

Ms. Macklin slightly rolled her eyes. "I'm embarrassed that you saw my performance. I wanted you to look up to me as your teacher, not to think I'm some kind of whore who will do whatever for money. That's not the case, and I have never had an intimate relationship with any man in that club. I make my money and go home."

"From what I saw, ma, that's hard to believe. But, then again, that's your business. I still respect you as my teacher, but I would be lyin' if I said I ain't been thinkin' about that night." I looked at her again, this time staring

into her eyes. "You're a very beautiful woman. I've always had some feelings for you, but I get the impression
that you think I be playin'."

"Jamal, having feelings for someone and just wanting to have sex with them are two different things. You
don't have feelings for me. Like most young men, all
you're thinking about is sex and who you're going to get
it from. Most of the time, after you get it, you move on
and stamp 'mission accomplished' on your foreheads. I
can't control your thoughts about me, but I would appreciate it if you never tell anyone what you saw that
night. I could lose my job, and I don't want the others
students viewing me as you probably already do."

"Your secret is safe with me. If I haven't said anything to anyone about you and Coach Johnson, then
you know I ain't gon' say nothin'."

She lowered her head and fumbled with her nails..

"Are you in love with him?" I asked.

She hesitated to answer, but did. "Yes, but . . ."

"But he's married, right?"

"I know, but that doesn't stop me from loving him.
We're working through some things right now, and
hopefully everything will work out."

I stood up and walked to the other end of the couch
where Ms. Macklin sat. "You deserve better," I said.
"Don't let no nigga feed you no bullshit about him
leavin' his wife. If I had to make you a bet, I'd say you're
wastin' your time."

Of course, she defended her situation. "Jamal, you
know nothing about my relationship with the coach.
I know what kind of future we have, and if I didn't, I
wouldn't have hung on for as long as I have."

I lifted her chin, as she hadn't even convinced herself. "Then you keep on *hangin'* on then, and if you
ever, ever think about just lettin' yourself loose and

havin' some fun, let me know. I know you think I'm such a young boy, but like you say, I don't know you; you don't know me either. I got mad feelings for you, and I can bust a nut anywhere. It would be nice, however, if I can combine all this shit I'm feelin', and lay it right into you."

Ms. Macklin seemed stunned by my bluntness. And when I leaned down to kiss her, I couldn't believe that she had accepted the taste of my tongue. Her hands touched the back of my head, pulling me closer to her as she leaned back on the couch. My stomach had tightened, and I couldn't believe that my hands were roaming on the sides of her legs. Our kissing had gotten even more intense, and my rock-hard dick was pressed into her hotspot. The pace of my heartbeat couldn't keep up with the anxiousness I felt, but her dog right next to us, barking its head off, was annoying.

"Ms. Macklin," I whispered between kisses. "Please get your dog."

Our intense kiss came to a halt. "Patrice," she said. "Call me Patrice, not ma."

I winked and smiled at her. "And, you can call me Prince."

We stared into each other's eyes for a few seconds, then Ms. Macklin reached down, touching my belt buckle. I swear I had already busted two, three, five nuts; I was just that anxious about getting inside of her.

"You gon' love this shit," I whispered while watching her pull my dick from my pants. It flopped out long, fat, and hard. She touched it, and the excitement in me was building by the second. I jumped up to remove my clothes, and Ms. Macklin slowly sat up. She covered her face with her hands and then rubbed her temples.

"What are we doing, Jamal? We can't do this."

"Oh, yes, we can," I said with my pants at my ankles.

Ms. Macklin grabbed my hand to stop me from getting undressed. "I'm sorry for doing this. But I . . . I think you should leave. This shouldn't have happened." She stood up, and when I hugged her waist, she turned away from me.

"Sex between us is goin' to happen. I can promise you that, ma. You can fight this all you want to, but you're wastin' your time. Let's just do this shit, all right? I swear I'll make it feel good, and I won't tell nobody."

She stood in thought, then eased away from my embrace to pick up her barking dog. Seeing that she was making her way to the door, I felt disappointed. I pulled up my pants and tightened my belt.

"I'm sorry," she said again, and as soon as she opened the door, we saw Coach Johnson standing on the porch, getting ready to knock. He stepped inside, looking at Ms. Macklin, who couldn't look into his eyes, and at me, who chose to stare him down.

"Did I interrupt something?" he asked.

Ms. Macklin started doing the same shit Mama did when she was busted, combing her hair back with her fingers. Too, she gave Coach Johnson a fake-ass smile, and hiked up on the tips of her toes to give him a kiss.

"No, you didn't interrupt anything. I just wanted to talk to Jamal about Romeo and about us. He understands that he's not supposed to tell anyone."

Coach Johnson grinned and rubbed his goatee. He stepped farther into the living room, and held out his hand for me to shake it.

"Are you playin' in the game this weekend?" he asked. "You know we miss you."

I looked at his hand, and left him hanging. At that moment, I couldn't stand his ass, nor did I want to play on the team that he was coaching. I told Ms. Macklin to have a good night. Even though I knew that sly mutha-fucka was about to dig deep into my woman, I also felt that my day was coming too.

Finally, I'd gotten a call from Romeo. I accepted the charges. It was good to finally hear my partna speak on the other end.

"What's up?" was the first thing I said, with a huge grin on my face.

"A whole lot." He sounded upbeat. "But I don't have a lot of time to explain. I'm expected to go before the judge next week, and I'm hopin' he'll set a low bond for me. The public defender said that they'd have to prove that I was the one who pulled the trigger. Ain't nothin' tyin' me to that gun, and if anything, I may be charged with being an accessory to the crime. It looks like I may get minimal time, maybe just a few months, especially because of my age. That may be a good thing. Nobody in here thinks I'll be lookin' at life or anything like that."

I felt relieved. "That's good. Man, I wish you would have gone with me that night. I can't wait to tell you about all that's been going on. Make sure you let me know what's up with court and you know I'll be there."

"I'll call you the early part of next week. In the mean-time, call my grandmother and let her know what's up. I may need her to see what she can do for me money-wise on her end, 'cause I don't know if I can trust a public defender. See what you can come up with, too."

"All right, man. Be easy and I'll see you next week."

Later that day I walked to Romeo's house to talk to his grandmother. The smile on her face implied that she was happy to see me, but when we got into the kitchen where she was stirring a pot of greens, I wasn't sure. I told her what Romeo said and she let me have it.

"A public defender ain't gon' do nothing for that boy. They didn't do nothin' for his mama and they damn sure ain't gon' do nothin' for him. He should have known better than to go out and do something so stupid, but Romeo been messing around like that for years. I told him his mess was going to catch up with him, but he didn't listen. Y'all never, ever do, until it's too late."

His grandmother wiped her wrinkly hands on her apron and slowly scooted over to the table with me. She had a slight stench on her, and it was the smell of urine. I felt so sorry for her, and it looked as if she was barely hanging on. I helped her into the chair. She then picked up an apple from the table and started slicing it.

"Do you think you'll be able to go to court with me next week? I'm ridin' the MetroLink downtown to the courthouse."

"I'm not sure what I'm going to do, Jamal. I'm getting tired of running, trying to save these kids. I've been running all of my life. I don't have any money to put up for no bond and this house ain't worth nothin'. Even if it was, this is all I got. I put up my house before for Romeo's mother, and almost lost it. I tell you, boy, that I am sick to the pit of my stomach. I thought Romeo would turn out better than all the others. He had no business in those white folks' house tryin' to take nothin'. They gon' make an example out of him, you wait and see. They waiting for boys like you and Romeo to get caught up, and when you stay in the streets like y'all do, you're only asking for trouble."

I was quiet and let Romeo's grandmother speak her piece. Many tears flowed from her eyes, and I reached over to hug her several times. She truly wanted the best for Romeo, but, according to her, it was too late for him. She wasn't sure if she was going to court, but she told me it depended on how she felt.

Chapter 9

Things around my house were pretty sticky. Mama wasn't saying much to me, and she had expressed her disappointment in me. She was upset because I hadn't injected myself into her and Raylo's argument. I reminded her what doing so had gotten me in the past—stabbed. With that, she threw her hand back, calling me all kinds of names and telling me that I was no longer her son. I knew she was mad because Raylo hadn't come back since, so I didn't trip. I stayed in my room, thinking about my progress with Ms. Macklin and Romeo. His court date was in a few days. He asked if I was able to come up with any money, and he also told me to go back to his grandmother's house to get his car. I had no way of getting the kind of money he'd probably need, but I did have one option. I knew Mama told me never to go to Derrick for money, but I was desperate. I knew where I could find him, so I drove to his house, in hopes that he would come through for me this time.

After ringing the doorbell several times, a beautiful young woman, looking to be in her mid-twenties, opened the door. She asked who I was, and when I told her that I was Derrick's son, she let me inside. From the outside, I could tell the two-story house was dope, but the inside was off the chain. It was decorated with all black furniture and white accessories. I could see my image in the mirror-like white marble floors, and an L-shaped staircase led to the upper level. My so-called father was living it up; compared to this house, the house that Mama and I lived in was like living in hell.

The woman invited me to take a seat on the black leather sofa, and then she turned on a plasma TV that was above a lit fireplace.

"I'll let Derrick know that you're here. Is he expecting you?"

"No. No, but I have somethin' important I'd like to talk to him about."

She left the room and left me sitting there, mesmerized by the high, vaulted ceilings, the circular fish tank, and tall, glass-arched windows that gave a view of the backyard. An Olympic-sized swimming pool was in my view, and there were acres of nothing but land. Minutes later, Derrick strutted into the room, smiling as he talked to someone on the phone. When he saw me, his smile vanished and he ended his call. He gathered his black silk robe, tying it tighter before he took a seat.

"I need to remind that skeeza she can't open the door and let anyone into my house. Why are you here?" he asked.

I couldn't believe how nervous I was. Being around him made me feel that way. I rubbed my sweating hands together and was straightforward with him.

"I came here to get a loan. My friend, Romeo, got into some trouble and he may need a couple . . . several grand to get out of jail. I wondered if you could help me."

Derrick slightly grinned and leaned back farther on the couch. "You couldn't be serious, could you?"

"I'm dead serious. I wouldn't be here if I wasn't. I know you got this thing where you don't want shit to do with me, and I'm cool with that. But I didn't have nowhere else to turn. If I didn't have to be here, I wouldn't have come."

Derrick stared at me before responding. "You . . . you know what I don't like about you, nigga? I don't like that you judged me before knowin' anything about me. For years, you listened to that bitch-ass mother of yours, and every time I saw you on the streets, you treated me ill. It wasn't that I turned my back on you, fool. You turned your back on me. Your mama fed you all that bullshit over the years, and when I was tryin' to make shit right, she was up in another nigga's face. I washed my hands of her ass, and of you. It's too late for me to play Daddy, and, quite frankly, I don't have time for it. You're a grown-ass man now, doing shit how you wanna do it. I'm sure that fool Raylo has been takin' good care of you. I don't understand why you're at my fuckin' house, and not at his."

I frowned, and raised my voice. "Look, I don't give a rat's ass what went down between you and my mama. All I know is I've been the muthafucka left without. I am doin' things my way, but it doesn't mean that I won't reach out if need be. Now, can you help me with this shit or not? If not, say so and I'll get the fuck out of here."

Derrick gazed over at me with a twitching eye. "If I give you a loan, just how do you intend to pay me back?"

I shrugged, not even thinking about paying him back. "I'm not sure, but over time, I'm sure I can do a bit of husslin' and get your money back to you."

"Are you willin' to move some shit around for me? I got all kinds of li'l bricklayers out there for me, helpin' me build my empire. You can get on the payroll too, and if you're over here tryin' to borrow some money, then I suggest you consider helpin' me too."

"I ain't tryin' to do it like that. I'm workin' on gettin' my boy out of jail, not tryin' to make a way for me to get behind bars. Like I said, I got other ways of payin' you back, just not slingin' no dope."

Derrick's cell phone rang, and when he looked to see who it was, he left the room. I waited for about fifteen minutes before he came back into the room with an envelope in his hand. He handed it to me.

"I'm not sure how much you need for your partna, but this is all I can spare. Make sure I get every dime of it back. The next time you decide to pop up like this, your entry will be blocked."

I took the fat envelope from Derrick's hand, wanting to shake it, but didn't. Instead, I thanked him, and then turned to him before I walked out the door.

"I will see to it that you get this back. I'll send someone to bring it to you, especially since I'm not welcome."

Derrick nodded. I left, and couldn't wait to get inside of the car to see how much it was. I tore open the envelope and couldn't believe my eyes. I couldn't believe how many bills there were. He had given me a whopping fifty dollars, and had the audacity to ask for it back. I could have gotten out of the car to kick his ass, and after sitting for a few minutes, that's exactly what I decided to do. I rushed to the door, and kept buzzing the doorbell like I was crazy. This time, no one came to the door.

"Answer the door, you sly-ass muthafucka," I yelled. "Is this how you gon' play me?"

I got no answer, so instead of ringing the doorbell, I started banging on the door with my fist. "Come outside so I can kick yo' ass! You ain't shit, man, I swear yo' ass ain't nothin'!"

I threw the envelope at the door, and the bills floated to the ground. As I started to walk away, I picked the biggest rock I could find in his landscaping setup, and tossed it into a window. Glass shattered everywhere. I figured that would get his attention. I rushed to Romeo's car to get my Glock from underneath the seat. As soon as I backed out of the car with it, Derrick was standing in the doorway with a 9 mm in his hand. I aimed my gun in his direction.

"Punk-ass muthafucka," he spat. "If you shoot, you'd betta not miss. Now, I gave you all that I'm gon' give you, so you'd betta get in that piece of shit–ass car and get it off my property before yo' mama be buryin' yo' ass."

I sucked my teeth, knowing that I could take him out in an instant. Without saying a word, I tossed my gun on the front seat of Romeo's car and slowly walked toward the door. My eyes stared deeply into Derrick's, and not once did I look at the gun that was still aimed at me. I stepped up close to Derrick, then put his gun on my heaving chest.

"Stop talkin' that bullshit and put me out of my misery. If not, I swear to you that I am goin' to be your worst fuckin' enemy. You got your chance, today, to settle this, and if you don't, I will never, ever give you this chance again."

Derrick's eye twitched again, and he slowly removed the gun from my chest. He said nothing else to me, and after a few more seconds of being stared down, he went back into the house, slamming the door behind him.

Ol' punk-ass fool, I thought. Not only was he not man enough to take care of me, but he wasn't even man enough to kill his number-one enemy. I was sure the day would come when he wished he had.

Romeo's arraignment was on Tuesday, so I had missed another day of school. I couldn't wait to get to school yesterday, only to find that Ms. Macklin had called in sick. That really messed up my day. I hoped that she got well soon. Coach Johnson was real short with me during practice, but I didn't trip. It did me good to let out some steam, and the best way to do it was during practice.

When Tuesday rolled around, I called Romeo's grandmother to see if she was going to court with me. She didn't answer her phone, and when I stopped by her house, she didn't open her door. People were killing me with that shit. If you didn't want to be bothered by someone, then just open the damn door and say so. I left, just so I could make it to court on time.

Surprisingly, the courtroom wasn't as crowded as I expected it to be. There were a bunch of uppity lawyers walking around, whispering to each other, and several people sat spaced out on the wooden benches. I sat in the far back, eyeballing everyone who came through the door, and everyone who left. The judge came in, and everyone was asked to rise. I stayed in my muthafucking seat, and bent down as if I were busy tying my tennis shoes. I wasn't sure if anyone noticed, and, quite frankly, I didn't care.

The judge took his seat, and about thirty minutes later Romeo came out and stood before the judge. He was handcuffed, his hair was nappy as hell, and it looked like he hadn't showered in weeks. When he spotted me he cracked a tiny smile. I knew he was disappointed that his grandmother wasn't there. He stood next to the public defender, and when the judge asked Romeo to state his full name, he also read the charges against him and asked for his plea. Romeo said his full name—Romeo Lee Robertson—and then pled not guilty. The prosecutor then went on to tell the judge why Romeo should be denied bond. The public defender argued that Romeo shouldn't. I guess it really didn't matter either way, as Romeo's grandmother wasn't putting up her house, nor was I capable of getting the kind of money he would possibly need to be free.

When all was said and done, the judge looked at Romeo with disgust and quickly made his decision. No bond would be set, he would be tried as an adult, and Romeo would remain in jail until his trial, which was scheduled in two months. Romeo turned to look at me, shaking his head. I cut my eyes at the judge, and before I said anything that got me in trouble, I rushed out of the courtroom. I put my hoodie over my head, realizing how much Mama's words made sense. The white man ran this shit, and there wasn't much especially a black young man like me could do about it.

No sooner had I walked through the door than the phone was ringing. Mama wasn't there. When I picked up the phone, it was Romeo. As always, he said that he didn't have much time to talk, but wanted me to talk to his grandmother about bringing him some money and books to read. He was disappointed that she hadn't come with me today, but I had no control over her decision. He then advised me not to worry about his case, but admitted to being afraid about what would happen. I told him that I was worried too, but would do my best to get some money and books to take to him. As soon as we ended our call, I grabbed the car keys so I could go see what was up with his grandmother. Romeo said that she hadn't been answering her phone, and it wasn't like her not to at least talk to him.

A bunch of cars were parked outside of Romeo's grandmother's house, and when I knocked on the door, his uncle came to it. Out of the five uncles that Romeo had, Trevor was the only decent one in the family. He stepped on the porch to talk to me.

"My mother isn't here," he said with a blank expression. "She died yesterday in her sleep, and my family is here to go over the arrangements. I know she was supposed to go to Romeo's arraignment today, and tell Romeo that I'm sorry, but . . ."

He got choked up and started to cry. I really didn't know what to say, but I knew the news would be another setback for Romeo. He loved his grandmother, and I was sure that he would feel as if her worries about him contributed to her death. I wasn't even sure if I would tell him, and, at this point, I was going to leave it up to his family to do so. I told Trevor how sorry I was for his loss, and left. I couldn't stop thinking about how, over the years, his grandmother had been nothing but nice to everyone. Thinking about her had me thinking about Mama. I hoped that our relationship didn't come to an abrupt end as this one had.

Mama hadn't been home all day. I was hungry again, but at least there was some bologna and cheese in the fridge for me to make a sandwich. I also made a pitcher of cherry Kool-Aid, then headed for my room to chow down. I sat on the floor with my PS3 controller in one hand and my sandwich in the other. My thoughts were about Romeo and his grandmother, but then I started to think about Ms. Macklin. I wanted to be alone with her again, and there was no way in hell I'd let her stop me again. I felt a bit let down. It had seemed as if the moment she got a glance at my dick, she shut me down. Maybe it wasn't big enough for her, or maybe my kissing techniques weren't right? Older women expected more from sex, and I had to admit that I wasn't always as creative as I could be. Most of the time, I found myself in stick-and-move situations. It was all about getting a nut, but I couldn't approach Ms. Macklin in that manner. I'd have to take my time with her, making sure that every inch of her body was satisfied. I had watched numerous porn movies in my day, but it was time for me to brush up. I took a few more bites of my sandwich, then looked in the closet for one of my porn DVDs. I put one in the DVD player, and began to take notes. I'd never eaten pussy, but the man in the video was fucking the woman with his curled, pointed tongue. I stuck out my tongue, trying to make it flow like his. The woman in the video was pulling her hair out, telling the man how spectacular his performance felt. I wanted to make Ms. Macklin feel that way, and as my tongue started to get into a rhythm, I looked in the mirror to see how I looked doing it. I closed my eyes, visualizing how pretty her pussy looked at the strip club that day. In my mind, I was tearing it up, too. I became even more anxious about being alone with her again.

I put my tongue back into my mouth, stroking my hardness down below. I was just about ready to get off, but the phone interrupted me. Without looking at the called ID, I answered.

"Jamal Perkins?" the stern voice on the other end asked.

"Yeah, who's callin?"

"This is Monesha's father. My daughter is pregnant, young man, and from my understanding, you're the father. You *need* to get with Monesha's mother and me, and tell us how you intend to take care of *your* baby."

"I don't need to do nothin'. You need to set up a spot for your daughter on the *Maury* show, because I am not the father of that baby. Until you have proof, don't call my house disrespectin' me no more."

I hung up. How dare Monesha's trifling ass try to put her baby off on me? These girls were proving themselves to be something else. Before it was all said and done, I was gon' have to hurt somebody for lying on me. I lay across my bed, and quickly got back to my thoughts of eating Ms. Macklin's pussy.

Chapter 10

Mama had been whack. We were constantly arguing about stupid shit, and since she didn't have Raylo around no more to gripe with, she turned her bullshit on me. I almost fucked her up last night, but instead I left the house and went to one of the football players' houses to chill. His name was Cedric, and I'd known him since elementary school. We hadn't gotten close until recently, and that was because Romeo wasn't around. Cedric was hooked up in some gang shit, but he always treated me with respect. Next to me, he was also good at playing football, so that's why we pretty much got along. Just this week, he and I had robbed a lady coming out of a bank that was near his house. She had over $1,600 on her, so we both split it. I went to go see Romeo, but they wouldn't let me see him because I was under-aged. They said I had to have a parent or guardian with me, but so much for that shit. Still, I left some money for him and some books to read. I had to coax a guard into letting me do that, but I guess she felt sorry for me. A few days later he wrote me, saying that he was bored out of his mind, and he thanked me for being there for him. He asked about his grandmother, but in the letter I wrote to him I simply told him that I couldn't get in touch with her. According to his letter, no one from Romeo's family had reached out to him, and I knew he felt alone. Hopefully, he knew he had a true friend in me, and forever would.

We were on winter break at school, and prior to that, Ms. Macklin had not been at school for two weeks. Football season had wrapped up, and we lost the last two games. I didn't even play in one of them, only because I wasn't feeling up to it. Coach Johnson wasn't the kind of man who inspired me, and he could tell that I wasn't feeling nothing about him. I had an awkward feeling that Ms. Macklin hadn't been to work because of him, and I had planned to drop by her place to see what was up.

For now, though, Christmas was next week and so was my birthday. Cedric and I were in the streets, straight up getting it done. We'd been to the mall, shoplifting our asses off. I had so much shit, and kept most of it at his house. My intention was to sell all of the items I'd gotten, and I'd already unloaded about two grand worth of merchandise to everyday, ordinary people on the streets. Between stealing at the stores, and robbing folks on parking lots, I barely had time to do anything else. Making money this way was a'ight, and the scared looks on people's faces were priceless. Everybody wanted to live, and it was all about calling on God. Cedric liked putting fear in people more than me, and as we sat in the car eyeballing this Uncle Tom–looking black man, we suspected he would be our next victim. He was busy on his cell phone, carrying numerous bags from shops at the mall. As soon as he clicked his chirper, we saw the lights to a black BMW come on. Cedric hopped out of the car, bumping the man's shoulder with his. The brotha took the phone away from his ear, irritated by the bump.

"Excuse you," he said to Cedric. "Didn't you feel how hard you bumped me?"

As the man's head was turned, I crept up on him. I cracked him upside his head with my Glock, and the abrupt blow sent him staggering to the ground. Cedric grabbed his bags, and as I tried to reach into his pockets for his wallet, he struggled with me. I punched his face, and I'd be damned if he didn't punch me back. I figured that the ongoing struggle would draw attention, and as I looked up, I saw two white women peeping over the cars to see what was up. They picked up their pace, I guess not making such a big deal of two black men fighting. Cedric thought fast, and when he placed his Glock against the man's temple, that's when the man calmed down and backed away from me. I stood, stumbling backward with his wallet in my hand.

"Don't shoot me, please," the man's voice shivered with his hands defensively held out.

I could see the fury in Cedric's eyes, and I ran off to get the car. After all of the begging and pleading the man had done, I heard the gunshots ring out like firecrackers. I saw the man's body drop to the ground, and sped up so Cedric could get in the car. He dove into the front seat and I skidded out of the parking lot.

At first, things were pretty quiet in the car. This was the first time we'd had to shoot somebody. I suspected that it wasn't Cedric's first time, as he seemed calm as ever. We drove back to his house, and searched through the bags and man's wallet. He had a measly twenty dollars, but lots of credit cards. Inside the bags were some cashmere sweaters, a pair of jeans, women's negligees, a pearl necklace, and some items for kids. Yeah, he was a family man, and the wedding band on his finger implied it. Cedric and I divvied up the items, and couldn't help but tune into the news, where the reporters were discussing what had happened at the mall. According to one reporter, the man was rushed to the hospital in critical condition. The police had no suspects or motive.

Cedric stood, sliding his Glock down his pants. "And they won't ever find any suspects or motives, either."

"Are you sure about that?" I said, somewhat on edge about somebody seeing us or getting the license plates on Romeo's car.

"Man, as long as it's a black person, the police don't give a damn. That's why I don't even fuck with white folks. They will hunt a nigga down if a person is white, but rarely catch a black man's killer."

I started thinking about Romeo's case, and what Cedric said was right. Nah, they didn't give a damn about that man and his family, and, obviously, neither did we. It was all about making money for me, and if somebody got hurt in the process, so be it. The man should have upped his shit without a fight. It's only when a nigga play gangsta that I gotta get gangsta back. That's what he got, and I damn sure wasn't gon' sit there and fight with his ass. That would have sparked more attention. The more I thought about it, the more I had to say that Cedric did the right thing to protect us.

My birthday had come and gone, and so had Christmas. I hadn't seen Mama in days, but she did call on Christmas morning to tell me she was at a friend's house and wasn't sure when she was coming home. She claimed she needed a break from the house, but that actually meant that she needed a break from me. I wished her a Merry Christmas and ended the call. She hadn't even called to wish me a happy birthday, but Romeo did. Our conversation was short, but it did me justice to hear his voice. He seemed a bit down, and was ready for his case to go to trial. We hoped for good news to come out of it, and with the truth being told, how could it not work out in his favor?

Nadine had also called on my birthday. She left a message on voice mail. I didn't call her back, as I didn't want her getting any ideas about me accepting the baby she was carrying. Some of the other chicks from my school had called too, and, just for the hell of it, I drove to Sabrina's house so I could get the birthday present she had waiting for me. This time, sex was better with Sabrina, especially tackling it without Romeo. I finally tried to experiment with eating pussy. It was okay, but Sabrina didn't have her stuff together like Ms. Macklin did. Her bush was too hairy and the Brillo Pad feeling had me thinking that I was gon' cut my lips. I went with the flow, simply because my performance had her screaming at the top of her lungs. She kept screaming my name, and I liked that shit. It let me know how much I was in control, and that was a good thing. Then again, maybe not. She had been working my nerves, begging for me to come over every day since then.

Today, however, I didn't have time. School was back in session in two days, and I wanted to see what was up with Ms. Macklin. I drove by her apartment, making sure that Coach Johnson was nowhere in sight. He wasn't, so I went to the door and knocked. Moments later, Ms. Macklin opened the door looking somber as ever. She didn't have on a drop of makeup, her hair was brushed back into a ponytail, and the smile I expected to see wasn't there.

"Jamal, what are you doing here?" she asked without inviting me inside.

I put my hands in my pockets, shivering from the cold and gusty wind.

"I just stopped by to check on you. You hadn't been to work, and I hope it didn't have anything to do with me."

"No," she said, widening the door. "Come in."

I was delighted that she invited me in, so I stepped inside and removed the hood from my new leather jacket. I followed Ms. Macklin into her spacious kitchen that was separated from the living room, but visible. She leaned against the counter with her arms folded, and I took a seat at the kitchen table.

"I don't like you showing up like this," she said. "But please don't think that my absences had anything to do with you."

"I apologize for poppin' up like this, ma, but I was worried about you. You'd been on my mind, and I figured you wasn't comin' to work because you were tryin' to avoid me."

Ms. Macklin rubbed her hair back with her hand, then tightened the belt on the pink silk robe she wore. It revealed her shapely, smooth legs. If only I could see, taste, and touch what was underneath. -

"I wasn't trying to avoid you. I was trying to avoid someone else. The situation with you hasn't helped me one bit, and I feel terrible about what happened the last time you were here. I crossed the line, Jamal, and I am deeply sorry for doing so. That should have never happened."

"I disagree, and there is nothin' that you can say to me to make me regret it. As for you tryin' to avoid someone, would that person be Coach Johnson?"

She hesitated to answer, but nodded.

"If you don't mind me askin', what's up with y'all? Why you always letting that nigga get you down?"

Ms. Macklin rubbed her forehead, then came over to the table to take a seat. She had a sad look on her face, and all she did was move her head from side to side. "Let's just say that I should have known better, Jamal. I've been making some really bad decisions, and getting myself involved with Coach Johnson was the worst thing I could have ever done."

"I don't mean to sound harsh or anything, but didn't you see this comin'? I mean, he's a married man, and married men always lie to their mistresses. You kind of come off as bein' naïve, and I hadn't pegged you as bein' that way."

She shrugged. "I thought I was in love with him. He told me that he and his wife were having major problems and they would soon be divorced. As much time as we spent together, I truly believed him. That is, until she followed him over here and he was forced to confront both of us together. Needless to say, he told me he'd made a mistake and he went home with his wife. I've called him several times for an explanation, but he won't even return my phone calls. I . . . I feel so betrayed and hurt." Ms. Macklin paused, taking a hard swallow. Her eyes watered, and she continued. "I thought he cared, but he obviously doesn't. I can't even look at him right now, and that's why I haven't been coming to work."

I was blunt. "That's stupid. Why you lettin' that nigga get to you like that and you got kids at that school countin' on you? Especially me. My motivation just ain't been the same. Honestly, I looked forward to seein' your pretty face every day."

I smiled, and, lucky for me, so did Ms. Macklin.

"Jamal, that's kind of you to say, but I don't want credit for motivating you. You have missed too many days of school, and with me there or not, you'd better start thinking about how you're going to make it out of that school."

"I've been thinkin' about it, but I'm tellin' the truth about how excited I be to see you. If you can promise me that you'll come back to work, then I can promise you that I'll show up every day, until the end of the year."

Ms. Macklin blushed, then playfully cut her eyes to look away. "I can't make you any promises, but we'll see how I'm feeling in two more days. School starts back then, and hopefully I'll be feeling better. For now, I need some time alone to clear my head and figure out what I need to do."

I slowly stood up, figuring that was my cue to leave. "I'll let you get your thoughts together, but I'd better see you at school, a'ight?"

She didn't respond. She got up from the chair, and moved toward the door to let me out. I followed close behind her, gazing at her plump ass, which was moving underneath her silk robe. *Damn, I wanted to fuck her so badly.* My dick was about to bust through my jeans. I could feel it pulsating. My anxiousness caused me to ease my arm around her waist before she opened the door. She quickly turned around, staring face-to-face with me.

"Jamal," she said.

"No. Prince. We're getting on a more personal level, wouldn't you say?"

She hated to grin, but did. "Prince, please don't touch me like that. You are taking us down a dangerous path, and I don't see anything good that can come of this."

I took a few steps forward, backing her up to the door. "I think you're so wrong about that. And, just for the record, my birthday just passed and I'm eighteen years old now. We can do this, and as soon as you get your head on straight, we will."

She shot me down by shaking her head. "No, we can't."

I ignored her rejection. "Can I have a birthday kiss, or do I have to take it?"

"Prince, stop," she said, placing her hand on my chest that had gotten closer to hers. "You don't under-stand how complicated . . ."

I leaned in to silence her words. My soft lips touched hers and she mumbled. A few seconds later, she was silent and the kissing became intense. So intense that she lifted her hand to rub the back of my head. I wanted her to feel my hardness, so I pushed it in her direction. My hands lowered to her ass, and just as I was getting ready to search underneath her robe, she grabbed my hands.

Our closed eyes popped open at the same time. "Happy belated birthday," she softly whispered. "Now leave."

Was she fucking teasing me or what? This shit wasn't going down like this. I was getting frustrated with her playing games. "What is up with you?" I asked in a begging and pleading manner. "You know how bad I want to do this shit, and you keep on playin' a nigga like you ain't feelin' him. You messin' with my self-esteem, and if you—"

Ms. Macklin held the sides of my face to shush me. "I'm under pressure right now, and I don't want to do something because I'm feeling hurt by someone else. Maybe our time together will come, but, please, not today. I don't want to put you in the middle of this. Go home, and enjoy your next few days off. I'll see you at school on Monday, okay?"

I was hypnotized by her presence, and all I could do was nod. She laid an even better kiss on me this time, then opened the door so I could leave. I felt like a zombie, waving good-bye and telling her that I'd see her soon.

On the drive home, my mind was cluttered with the thoughts of Ms. Macklin. She had me all fucked up, and I wanted to tell somebody what I was feeling. I hadn't even told Romeo about us yet, only because she had asked me not to say a word to anyone. Also, I didn't want him to feel bad about not having his freedom. I knew he was going crazy in jail, and the last time I'd spoken to him, he said just that.

On Monday, I was lucky that I had made it to school. Just last night there was a serious bloodbath in my hood. Niggas were dropping like flies, and steel had been slinging everywhere. The news was reporting one murder incident after another, all Black-on-Black crimes. The chief of police was even on TV asking people to please come forward if they knew anything about the crimes. So much for that, because in my hood, people weren't talking. No one wanted to be labeled as a snitch, and that in itself wasn't a good thing. I had been involved with two of the fights that occurred, but my Glock had been pulled on no one. Some dope-pushing fools from the other side of town tried to jump on Cedric as we'd left a music store. Cedric started spraying bullets and had every last one of those fools running for cover. There was no getting away from me, as I was an extremely fast runner. I caught up with two of the brothas, and once Cedric met up with us, we delivered a bone-crushing beating that they would never forget. I had so much anger built up inside of me, and it felt good to let out my frustrations. The two brothas lay there in a pool of blood. At that point, using a gun wasn't even necessary.

My fists had done the job I wanted them to do, and that usually meant that somebody had been knocked unconscious. Even so, before Cedric and I made it home on foot, we were approached by another gang of niggas. Being with Cedric was bringing out too much drama, and I kept thinking about what Mama had said about watching the company you keep. This time, I sprinted down an alley to get away, hiding behind every trash Dumpster I could find. The brothas in a silver Cadillac were casing the alley and streets all night, trying to find me or Cedric. He was long gone; I'd seen him hop a fence to get away. We'd spoken on the phone last night, and it was good to know that he was safe. He talked about me joining the north-side gang he was in, but I hadn't made a decision yet. I felt like I was living in another world without Romeo around, and even though I was happy about not hearing Mama's sassy voice, I kind of missed her being around, too. I always wanted to belong to a family who had my back, and for the last month or so, Cedric had shown me that he had the qualifications of being a brother. I told him I'd get back to him about my decision to join a gang.

Two days later, there I was laying my head on the table and waiting for Ms. Macklin to enter the class. She hadn't made it in yet, nor had a substitute teacher. Nadine kept eyeballing me. I guessed she was mad because I hadn't returned her phone calls. Sabrina was smiling at me, but there was only so much cheesing a brotha could take. That's why my head was on the table, and having my ear against my arm helped drown out some of the loud talking in the classroom. What seemed to be only minutes later, Ms. Macklin came in, carrying a bunch of books in her arms. I jumped up to help her, but she ordered me to sit down.

"As a matter of fact," she said, "please take a seat at one of the desks. You no longer have to sit at the table next to me."

I sat at the table, denying her request. "Nah, I'm good. I like where I'm at, that way I can stay out of trouble."

Ms. Macklin didn't respond. She placed the books on her desk and shouted for the students to be quiet. The room went silent.

"Thank you," she said, walking around to the front of her desk. She wore a khaki wrapped dress with high-heeled brown shoes. When she sat on top of her desk, she crossed her legs, displaying nothing but sexiness. I caught a side view of her, so maybe it was in my best interest to take a seat at one of the desks. I stood to go find the closest desk to the front.

"Prince—I mean, Jamal—what are you doing?" she asked.

"I'm findin' me a seat, *ma*," I said, sitting at an empty desk that was in the third row, second seat. She waited until I was seated, then turned her attention back to the class.

"Okay," she sighed. "Has everyone been keeping up with the homework the substitute teacher gave you?"

More "no's" rang out than "yes's." I was a definite no.

"How come?" Ms. Macklin asked. "Just because I'm not here, it doesn't mean you all don't have to do your work."

One of the cheerleaders, Elin, raised her hand. "Ms. Macklin, no offense to the substitute, but she didn't explain stuff like you do. I couldn't understand what she was saying, and she spent most of her time in here reading magazines."

Many people agreed. No matter what, Ms. Macklin continued to counsel us on how important it was for us to at least try to do it. Her words sounded like mumbo jumbo to me, and all I could do was sit there and scan my eyes up and down her legs. *Damn*, I thought. *I actually know what her pussy looks like.* I envisioned myself being inside of it, and, while deep in thought, I twirled around the new diamond-studded earring in my ear with my finger. I kept wetting my lips and rubbing my low waves that were cut and trimmed to perfection by a skilled barber. I couldn't return to school looking like no bum, so I was decked out in Rocawear gear from head to toe. Ms. Macklin seemed to appreciate my look, and every chance she got, she glanced in my direction. This shit was definitely working in my favor, and when she had mistakenly called me Prince, I knew she would soon be on my team. She went over several algebra equations on the board, then assigned us two pages to complete. For those who had done work in her absence, she advised them to turn in their papers for a grade and extra credit. Three measly people rushed up to her desk to turn in their papers, one being Nadine. Her belly was growing by the day, and when she looked at me, I turned my head in another direction.

After the students took their seats, I went back to the table and sat near Ms. Macklin. She must have expected me to do so, and didn't even look up. I started on my assignment, and before I knew it, the bell was ringing. Everyone rushed to close their books, and broke out toward the door so they could go. I took my time, and as Sabrina slowly made her way to the door, I followed her.

Ms. Macklin called my name. "Jamal." I turned. She held a red envelope in her hand. "Take this," she said.

I walked up to her, taking the envelope from her hand. "What's this?"

"It's a birthday card, wishing you a happy one and thanking you for encouraging me to return to school. Now, go. I don't want you late for your next class."

I was on cloud muthafuckin' nine. I smiled, and moved a tad bit closer to her.

"Thanks," I whispered. "Can I have another one of those kisses, though?"

She backed up. "No, and I mean it. Not here."

Never doing as I was told, I quickly smacked her lips and backed my way to the door. Our eyes stayed connected until I walked out of the door and made my way to my locker. I quickly opened the card to see what Ms. Macklin had written inside. It read, HAPPY BIRTHDAY, PRINCE. THANKS FOR BEING THE KIND OF FRIEND YOU ARE, AND GOD BLESS YOU. IF YOU'RE NOT TOO BUSY THIS WEEKEND, I NEED HELP PAINTING MY APARTMENT. STOP BY AROUND NOON ON SATURDAY.

The card wasn't signed, but that didn't matter. I knew who it was from and I could finally tell what she really wanted.

Later that day, I sat in the cafeteria with Cedric and the rest of the football players. Our table was loud as ever, and we were talking about everybody and their mamas who came through the door. When Ms. Macklin came in, the fellas started talking shit. Everybody wanted to get hooked up, but little did they know I was getting so very close. I wanted to tell my secret, but I knew how much trouble it would cause her. She purposely walked by our table, and when Cedric called out her name, she turned.

"Yes, Cedric," she said, with all eyes on her.

"I . . . I was wonderin' if you would find time in your busy schedule to tutor me after hours. A brotha need some help, and the last time I checked, it was your duty to, uh, help a brotha out, right?"

"No, my duty is to help those who want to be helped. The last time I checked, you dropped my class and haven't been back since. I suggest you find yourself another tutor, Cedric, and good luck on doing so."

She walked away, and "dang's" and "ooh's" rang out. Cedric felt like shit and threw his hand back at her. "Man, fuck her. She ain't uppin' none of that anyway, and I bet her ass hollerin' for a man to blow her back out."

I made no comment, and got back to my conversation with the fellas. I kept my eyes on Ms. Macklin, though, and when Coach Johnson entered the cafeteria, I saw them look at each other. He nudged his head, and a few minutes later, he left the cafeteria. Minutes following, she left. Just for the hell of it, I got up to be nosey. But as soon as I dumped my tray, Nadine approached me, holding up two fingers.

"Can you find two minutes for me? I have something that I need to say to you, and I'll be done with it."

I was in a rush to see where Ms. Macklin and Coach Johnson had gone to, but I knew Nadine wouldn't let it go. We stepped outside of the cafeteria and I eased my hands in my pockets to listen.

"Speak," I said, displaying irritation on my face.

"I've been thinking about quitting school. My mama said I'll have to find a job to help take care of the baby, and since she works, I don't know if I'll have anyone to keep him. A few weeks ago, I found out it was a boy, and it would really mean a lot to me if you would consider helping me take care of him."

My face fell flat. I didn't understand why this chick kept sweating me. I wasn't even sure if the baby was mine, so for now I had nothing to offer her. "If you gotta quit school, then do it. Like I said before, I don't know who the father of your baby is, and I ain't claimin' nothin' until I'm one hundred percent sure. Stop fuckin' harrassin' me about this shit. I'm just about tired of hearin' it."

Nadine's brows went up and I swear she almost looked like the devil. "Harassing you," she shouted with tears rushing up to her eyes. "I've barely said anything to you about this baby. I'm trying to deal with this by myself, Prince, but why should I have to? You know damn well that you're the father, and you weren't talking all this ill shit when you were fucking me, were you? You need to man up and take care of your goddamn responsibilities! I shouldn't have to suffer like this. You have no idea what I've been going through."

People were starting to look at us, and, like always, I hated to feel embarrassed. I cocked my head from side to side and sucked my teeth. "I don't give a fuck what you've been going through, girl. To hell with you and that baby. You—"

Nadine caught me off guard and slapped the shit out of me. My cheek burned and I knew there was a handprint on it. My reflexes jumped, and before I knew it, she was against the wall getting the shit choked out of her. "You fuckin' bitch!" I said, seething with anger. I was just about ready to tear her ass up, until Cedric pulled me off her. She gagged, coughing and screaming at the same time.

"I hate you, Prince! I swear to God I hate you!"

Cedric was holding me back only a few feet away from her, and that's when she coughed out a gob of spit and spat in my face. I broke loose from Cedric's grip, only to be stopped in my tracks by six other football players who pushed me away from Nadine and held me back. She was being consoled by some of her girlfriends, and I did my best to break away from the numerous players' grips.

"Chill, Prince," one of the players said while gripping my neck. Two other players held my shoulders and one had my arm. I could feel Nadine's saliva sliding down the side of my face.

"You are lucky that I can't get to yo' ass right now," I shouted, and struggled to get away from the players' tight grips. Nadine had the nerve to taunt me while being pulled away by her friends.

"Nah, that's what you get! Bastard!"

"Let me the fuck go," I kept yelling. "I swear I'm gon' kill this bitch!"

The noise was too much for the teachers in the cafeteria, as well as for Coach Johnson and Ms. Macklin, who had come from nowhere. Ms. Macklin ordered Nadine's friends to take her to the principal's office. Coach Johnson called for the players to release me. They did, and I quickly wiped the spit from my face. Coach Johnson immediately reached for my arm, but I snatched it away. My face was still twisted from all that had happened.

"Get your hands off me," I snapped.

He didn't let go. "I'm taking you to the office. Let's go."

I snatched away from him again. "To the office for what? She the one who put her goddamn hands on me! I'm the muthafucka who got spit on and slapped. I didn't do nothin' to her ass, but I guess I'm gon' get suspended, too, right?"

"I didn't say that. All I'm saying is that you need to go to the office and cool down. Tell Mr. King what happened and ask him to question some of the students around here, so they can tell what happened. Now, if you'd rather stand here and argue with me, cool. Let's do it, but I guarantee you that you won't win an argument, nor a fight, with me."

Ms. Macklin stepped forward and reached her hand out to me. "Come with me," she said. "Let's go to the office to talk to Mr. King." She asked two of the other students to go with us, and as we made our way to the principal's office, they followed several feet behind us. I couldn't help but ask Ms. Macklin where she and Coach Johnson had gone.

"I'm not answering that right now," she said.

"Why not?"

"Because it's none of your business."

"I knew you would say that shit, ma. You got a smart-ass mouth too, and you'd better consider yourself lucky that it ain't my business. If it were, shit would be goin' down right about now."

Ms. Macklin halted her steps. She told the other students to meet us in the office and gave me a look that could kill.

"And what is that supposed to mean?" she shot back.

"Take it how you want to take it. Teach." I walked away.

She rushed up from behind and turned me to face her. "So, now you think that you have the right to disrespect me? Is that what you think?" I didn't respond. She pointed her finger at me and I could see the madness in her pretty eyes. "I am not like these little girls around here, Jamal, and you will not treat me as you do them. This is why I didn't want you in my business, and damn you for stirring up my feelings, only for you to turn around and treat me ill. I'll get someone else to help me paint my apartment, and, for now, you know what, Jamal? Screw you! Aside from that, stop referring to me as your darn ma. From now on, it's Ms. Macklin to you."

She switched her sassy and sexy ass away from me, and left me standing there with nothing to say in return. I couldn't believe that my own teacher had used that kind of language addressing me, but it was enough to make me chuckle. I heard someone clear his throat, and when I looked to see who it was, I saw it was Coach Johnson. He walked up to me, jiggling the change and keys in his pockets.

"Did, uh, I just hear something that I wasn't supposed to hear?" he asked.

I rubbed the minimal hair above my lip, hoping that he'd heard everything. "Depends on what you heard."

"Let's just say that I hope like hell you're not trying to move in on my territory. Are you?"

"Nah, not at all. Your territory resides at home with you, and I have no interest, whatsoever, in your wife."

"Jamal, don't bullshit me. You know damn well who I'm talking about, and for the record, she is not your type. Get your young mind out of the gutter. That's too much woman for you to handle. There's no need for you to be wasting your time."

I shook my head. "You know what? You mutha-fuckin' so-called-ass teachers in here puttin' on one hell of a front. I thought your job was to be teachin' me somethin'. Instead, you comin' at me about some bullshit over a woman who ain't even your wife. I can't believe you feel threatened by a young'un like me, but in this day and age, I understand. Don't nobody give a fuck anymore, and you, Coach Johnson, are a prime example of why niggas like me don't even go to school. In the meantime, don't trouble yourself about me and Ms. Macklin. She a straight dime, though, and for any-body to jerk her around, they must be one big-ass fool. Look in the mirror, Coach. You just may see yourself standin' there."

I calmly walked to the office to accept whatever pun-ishment Mr. King intended to lay on me. Surprisingly, he was easy on me, only because two other fights had broken out that day. One boy was badly injured and needed medical attention. Mr. King didn't have time to deal with my and Nadine's mess, and when all was said and done, Nadine was suspended for three days. I received no suspension at all. The other students told the truth about what had happened, and even though I had choked her, no one mentioned it. I looked like a victim, and that was, no doubt, a first for me.

Chapter 11

Mama was back at home with a new attitude. It didn't dawn on me as to why, until Raylo showed up on Friday night with a box of Kentucky Fried Chicken in his hand. This break-up-to-make-up shit was an ongoing thing. And no matter what they seemed to do to each other, they always managed to pull it back together. I wasn't feeling that kind of shit, and that's why having a relationship wasn't in my vocabulary. I wasn't trying to seriously hook up with anyone, and as much as I liked Ms. Macklin, I couldn't even see myself in a relationship with her. Yeah, the feelings were there, but my feelings were about getting some pussy. Nothing more, nothing less. I got the same vibes from her, and there was no way in hell she was even thinking about having a future with me. Even I didn't know where my future was headed, but I was starting to feel content with Cedric and some of his friends. They seemed to have my back, and made sure that I kept money in my pockets, clothes on my back, and food in my mouth. Mama had left my ass out there hanging, and I won't even mention my father. I saw his ass the other day, and he had the nerve to position his fingers like a gun and aim it at me. He definitely didn't know who he was fucking with, and with as much hatred as I had for his ass, he had better keep his distance.

Instead of robbing folks all the time, I wanted to find a job, but what some of the fast food joints were paying was ridiculous. I hadn't finished school yet, so working part time for minimum wage didn't seem logical. I couldn't get with that program; that kind of shit reminded me too much of slavery. All the white man needed to do was pull out his whip and get to cracking. Yeah, he was still slaving behind the scenes, but very few black folks were paying attention. I was alert, and, for now, I continued to make money the best way I knew how.

Romeo had three weeks to go before his court date, and on Saturday morning, I sat on my bed, writing him a long letter. I encouraged him to hang in there, but it didn't seem to be working. His letters were getting more and more depressing, and they actually made me feel depressed as well. I couldn't wait to see what happened. The jury had to get this shit right. I prayed that they would, and sealed Romeo's letter with my saliva. Afterward, I put on my baggy cargo pants with pockets and a white T-shirt. I cocked my New York Yankees hat to the side and grabbed the keys to Romeo's car so I could go do some painting.

After dropping Romeo's letter in the mailbox, I headed to Ms. Macklin's apartment. Yeah, she'd told me not to come, but I was sure she didn't mean it. Over the years, I had learned how forgiving women could be. Ms. Macklin didn't seem like the type to hold a grudge, and since she was going through some things with Coach Johnson, I intended to take advantage of her vulnerabilities. I knocked on her door, and from the outside I could hear loud music. I banged harder, and when the sound lowered, that's when she opened the door. She had on a pair of blue jean capris, a pink T-shirt, and a pink scarf was tied around her hair. Paint blotches were visible on her shirt, and a smudge of paint was on her cheek. She held a paint roller with bright yellow paint on it in her hand.

"What?" she scoffed.

"You asked me to help you paint and I'm here to help. Besides, it looks like you need it."

I stepped forward, causing Ms. Macklin to move aside. Nearly everything was covered with plastic, and she had made very little progress. I didn't care much for the loud yellow paint, but this was her place, not mine.

I tossed my jacket on the couch, and pulled my white T-shirt over my head. My perfectly cut body was on display, and all Ms. Macklin could do was stare.

"Where would you like me to start?" I asked.

She laid her roller on top of a paint can and folded her arms. "I really don't need your help, especially after how you spoke to me the other day."

I defensively held out my hands. "Sorry. Now, if you don't want to say shit else to me, cool. Just let me know where to get started and we can have this done in no time."

She rolled her eyes and bent down to pick up the roller. "You're such a smart ass. I can't believe how I let you work my nerves." She handed the roller to me and pointed to the far corner of the living room. "Start over there. I hope you know what you're doing. Please take your time. Everything is covered with plastic, but try not to drip any paint on the floors."

I took the roller from her hand. "Where's your dog? Did you cover her with plastic too?"

She wanted to smile, but wouldn't let herself do it. "No. That dog belonged to my best friend. I was just dog sitting that day."

I nodded and bobbed my head to T-Pain's music in the background. Before I got started, I cranked up the music and got busy.

It took less than an hour for Ms. Macklin and me to almost finish the living room. I was standing on a ladder, carefully working the high corners with a paintbrush. Ms. Macklin was touching up while singing Alicia Keys's version of "Empire State of Mind" by Jay-Z. She was all in it, kept putting her hands in the air, looking cute as ever. I knew Jay-Z's version, so I kicked it down. We couldn't help but smile at each other throughout the performance. When the song came off, she lowered the volume and plopped down on the covered couch.

"You don't know anything about that song." She laughed.

"Please," I said. Every song Jay-Z had was hooked up on my iPod, and I could rap them backward if I wanted to. "If anything, you don't know nothin' 'bout that."

I stepped down from the ladder, slightly pulling up my baggy pants that hung low on my waist. Sweat dripped from my body, and just by the look in Ms. Macklin's eyes, I could see how much she admired it. I placed the paintbrush on the can and sat next to her to take a break.

"I don't know why you're looking all tired and lazy. We still have my bedroom to do, as well as my two bathrooms," she said.

I looked around at the bright-ass living room, squinting from the awfully loud color. "I hope you're not stickin' with the same color. I'm not sure if I'm feelin' this."

She looked around at the room. "I think it looks nice. I like to wake up to things that brighten my day, and this room will do that for me. The other rooms will be colored the same, so when you get rested, I'll meet you in my bedroom."

She got off the couch, heading for her room.

"How much are you payin' me for this?" I yelled. "You never told me."

She came from the other room and stood with the brush in her hand. "I never told you because I thought you'd help me out for free. Was I wrong for assuming?"

"Very wrong," I said, getting off the couch. "There's always a price for everything."

Her brows went up and she went back into her room. I followed, and just like the furniture in the living room, her bedroom furniture had been covered with plastic. The room was much smaller, so I anticipated that it wouldn't take us that long. I left to crank up the music again, and then we got busy on her bedroom. This time, my body kicked up a major sweat in the cramped and stuffy room. I was hot as hell, and kept wiping sweat from my forehead.

"Damn," I said. "Why don't you turn the heat off and crack open some of these windows? It's hot as hell in here."

Ms. Macklin just looked at me and smiled. She covered her mouth and started to crack up. When I looked in the mirror to see what was so funny, I saw that I had smeared yellow paint on my forehead. I rubbed it to wipe it off, but that only made matters worse. She laughed again.

"Aw, okay," I said. "You think this shit real funny, don't you?"

I stepped away from the mirror and dipped my brush in the can of paint. I started toward Ms. Macklin and I'd be damned if she wasn't laughing anymore.

"Prince, don't play," she said with a serious look. "You are going to mess up my room. I can't afford to have paint all over the place."

"Who said anything about puttin' this anywhere in your room?" I got closer.

"Don't put that on me," she said, defending herself with her paintbrush. I couldn't help but pat her cheek with the brush, and she tore me up with hers as well. We made one big mess, but most of the paint was on us.

"I could kill you," she said, looking down at her pink shirt and capris. Paint was all over her clothes, but most of the paint was on my bare chest and arms. She gave me a wet towel to wipe off the paint. As we stood in her room, looking at the mess we'd made on the floor, she shook her head.

"It is going to take hours for us to clean this up. You'd better help me, too."

She walked to the side of her bed, and bent down to pick up a paintbrush that had been dropped on her hardwood floor. When she turned around, I eased my arm around her waist.

"I can think of somethin' better we can do for the next few hours. What about you?"

Ms. Macklin looked into my eyes, keeping my arms around her waist. She ran her finger over my chest, particularly tracing my Street Soldier tattoo. "I can think of some things too, Soldier Boy. Let's see who can be more creative."

I heard a thud when her paintbrush hit the floor. She threw her arms around my neck. As we kissed, I backed her up to the bed covered with plastic. The queen bed sat rather high off the floor, but I had no complaints. I would fuck her in an alley with rodents and still be satisfied. I kneeled between Ms. Macklin's legs, tugging at the zipper on her capris, as she tore at the zipper on my pants. There became a sudden rush to get each other naked, and between the disappearing clothes act, we continued to take lengthy, juicy kisses.

"I want this," she admitted while tightly gripping the muscles in my ass. "I've always wanted this to happen."

I couldn't believe she had finally admitted it, and her admission caused my dick to swell to capacity. It couldn't get any harder or bigger than what was already on display.

"You already know how much I wanted this, ma, and please, please don't back out of this shit right now," I said. "It . . . it's okay that I call you 'ma' again, right?"

"You can call me whatever you'd like to. As long as you don't call me a bitch."

I definitely couldn't promise her that, and only time would tell if I'd ever have to go there. For now, she was too busy confirming her words about how much she had always wanted this to happen, especially when she lay back on the bed in nothing but her skin. I couldn't believe how perfect and thick her body was, and she, indeed, had the prettiest titties and pussy my young eyes had ever seen. I wanted to explore her insides with my tongue, but a woman this bad had me nervous as hell. I wasn't even sure if I was sucking her titties correctly, but I took my time and did my best. Her legs were wrapped around my back, and I could feel the warmth coming from in between them. I wanted to dive right into it, but I kept reminding myself not to show anxiousness. Just like the man in the porn movie, I massaged her breasts and pecked my lips down her stomach. I licked around her navel with my pointed tongue, caressing her down to the tip of her hairless slit. Using my fingers, I popped her slit wide open, exposing a cherry drop that looked to be delicious and sweet. Ms. Macklin hadn't said one word, but her trembling sweaty stomach heaved up and down. Taking my chances, I dropped my face into it, diving tongue first. I kept turning her clit with my tongue, then dipped it into her insides as far as my tongue would go. Her legs had already dropped from my waist and she had them wide open. I felt like I was dreaming. She put a high arch in her back and her moans picked up. All she had to do was say my name, just so I could know this shit was on!

"Prince," she groaned. "Lick it dry, baby! Lick me *dry,"* she whined.

Wow, I was thinking with my eyes closed. *Is this my teacher?* She was my lover for now, and as she started to breathe more heavily, I slowly opened my eyes. White cream rushed from her insides, and I caught every single drop in my mouth. She went crazy on me, and when she jerked herself up, that's when I stopped. She pulled my face to hers, kissing me as if my performance satisfied her.

"Look on my dresser and get a condom," she said.

I did, and as I was putting it on, she eased off the bed and stood in front of me. Her back faced me, but her head was turned sideways so we could kiss.

"I didn't know you were talented like that," she said, taking my hands and assisting me with rubbing her melon-sized breasts. "That felt good. Now, show me what else you can do."

Ms. Macklin bent over on the bed, resting one of her legs on top of it. I stood from behind, taking in a view of her ass that was breathtaking. I couldn't wait to get inside of her, but as soon as I eased in, my body weakened. My legs almost buckled and I had to quickly regroup. She allowed me no time to do so, and the faster she backed that ass up against me, the more I wanted to explode. I felt weak. The inside of a pussy never, ever felt this good. I tightened my eyes, and squeezed my fingers into her hips.

"Goddamn!" I screamed out. "Slow this shit down, ma, please!"

She ignored me, and kept tossing it back to me faster and faster. I did my best to hang with her, and hoped that the muscles in my legs would stay strong. I tightened my ass, and as I started to throw it back her way, she slowed her pace.

"Yeah, that's what I'm talkin' about," I boasted. "You feelin' that shit now, ain't you?"

With every thrust, Ms. Macklin gasped for air. Our sweaty, naked bodies slapped against each other at a rhythmic pace. We connected better than I thought we would. Taking in the feeling, her eyes were closed and her bottom lip was occasionally being sucked into her mouth. She pulled her long, wet hair aside and started talking to me again.

"Fuck me *harder*, Prince." Her voice was strained. "Please, please, don't tell anyone that you fucked me like this."

"My lips are sealed," I said, unable to hold on any longer. Before I came, though, Ms. Macklin moved forward, causing me to flop out of her soaking wet, deep tunnel. She ordered me on the bed, and when I lay on my back, she straddled my lap. I didn't think this could cause my heart to race any more, but as soon as she started to ride me, it was over. I was on the verge of a major eruption and my whole body tightened. Never in a million years did I expect sex with a woman to feel this good. For years, I hadn't been doing nothing but playing around. Ms. Macklin kept bouncing up and down on me, turning herself in a circular motion and allowing me to see my entries as she stroked me. I was spent, and basically had nothing else to give. I quickly sat up, dropping my head back in defeat.

Once it was over, I wrapped my arms around her waist and we sat in silence for a few minutes. That was, until I had gathered enough strength to speak.

"I can't believe you got at me like that," I said, still a bit out of breath. "I hope I didn't let you down."

Ms. Macklin rested her arms on my shoulders. She gazed into my eyes with the most seductive stare ever and smiled.

"I needed exactly what you gave me," she said. "So, no, I was in no way disappointed. Surprised, more like it. Now I see why the girls at school make such a big fuss over you."

I was relieved to hear she was pleased. I'd never been required to step up my game like this, and if any of the chicks from school ever wanted to get with me again, then they had to be willing to put it down like Ms. Macklin. She was one bad chick!

Chapter 12

I was a street soldier on a mission, and after I tapped into Ms. Macklin, it was now mission accomplished. I had never, ever been so motivated about going to school, until now. Seeing Ms. Macklin every day was a pleasure, but we couldn't seem to get our act together during class. Either she was looking in my direction, or I was gazing at her, thinking about the unforgettable ride she'd given me. I hadn't revisited her, but it was definitely on my agenda. She had a very high sex drive, but I didn't mind one bit.

Even my attitude toward people had changed. I seemed happier and didn't let too much shit get to me. Mama and I were on better terms, and even when she started bitching, I kept my mouth shut and eliminated the back talk. It was amazing what good pussy could do for you, especially if it was given to you by a teacher who so many young men at my school desired. Cedric was a little upset that I had cut back on chilling with him, but I told him I met a chick from East St. Louis who had been keeping me busy. He definitely understood, and told me when I had time to stop by his crib.

As for the chicks around school, they were on the back burner. I heard all the gripes, but, again, I let that shit roll off my back. I even spoke to Nadine the other day, but, unfortunately, she rolled her eyes and kept on moving. Can't say that I didn't try, but that's just how *some* people were.

I was on my way to sixth hour when Sabrina approached me, jogging up the steps.

"You got a minute?" she said.

I knew the bell was about to ring, but I gave her the minute she'd asked for. "Yeah, what's up?"

"I'm not trying to get up in your business or anything, but are you involved with Ms. Macklin? I've been checking y'all out in class, and, lately, y'all been seeming awfully friendly with each other. I'm not the only one who thinks so. Some other people in the classroom noticed it too."

"People always around here startin' rumors. Does Ms. Macklin look like the kind of teacher who would have sex with me? Hell, no. Per my mama's request, Ms. Macklin's been tutorin' me, and I appreciate her tryin' to help me get out of this muthafuckin' school. So tell your cacklin'-ass friends in our classroom that they are readin' too much into what's really goin' on. I'd hate for Ms. Macklin to get in trouble for a bunch of lies and assumptions. So I suggest you quickly clear up any and all false rumors."

I started to step away from Sabrina, but she grabbed my hand. "I can do that, but I need to know why you don't call me anymore. I thought we were cool."

"We are. I'm just takin' it easy and tryin' to get focused on school, that's all. I got all kinds of people runnin' around here, claimin' they pregnant, and I don't need the hassles right now. I'm sure you understand how important school is to me right now, and until I bring up my grades, I ain't thinkin' about bein' with nobody. We still cool, but, no offense, I'm tryin' to lay low for a while."

"That's cool. Just get at me when you can."

I told her I would, and ran down the hall to sixth hour before the bell rang. I couldn't believe that bullshit I'd told Sabrina, but I wanted to cool the rumors about me and Ms. Macklin. We'd already talked about what to say to people if they asked. Whether we liked it or not, the rumors were bound to pick up.

I fell asleep during six hour, and, as I looked up to yawn, I spotted Coach Johnson looking into my class-room. He opened the door, and politely asked my teacher if he could have a moment with me. I wasn't in the mood to argue with him about Ms. Macklin, and the stares he'd been given me all week were laughable. I stepped into the hallway, yawning again from the lack of sleep I'd been getting.

"What's up?" I said, leaning against the lockers with my hands in my pockets.

He rubbed his goatee and hesitated before talking to me. "Let . . . let's go to my office. What I have to say can't be said out here in the open."

I followed Coach Johnson, dragging my feet. We stepped into his office and he closed the door, locking it behind him. I plopped down in the seat, but before my butt got comfortable, he grabbed me by my shirt and pushed me against the door. Without saying a word, his fists tightened. He swung at me, but I ducked. I charged at him, grabbing his waist and slamming him back on his desk. Papers scattered everywhere, and when I jumped on him, we both fell to the floor. His powerful fists were slamming into my ribs, and I was throwing blows at him everywhere I could. That was, until the bitch-ass nigga karate kicked me between my legs. I grabbed my dick and lay back on the floor. I swayed from left to right, trying to calm the excruciat-ing pain between my legs. My balls were stinging so bad, they felt as if they were bleeding.

"*Shit,*" I shouted as water rushed to my eyes. I tight-ened them and turned my body in a cradled position.

Coach Johnson stood over me, wiping the minimal blood from his lip. He pointed his finger at me. "Let me know when you want to talk again, all right?"

He opened the door. "Soon, muthafucka!" I yelled. "Real soon!"

Romeo's trial had lasted for three days. I missed three half-days of school, but, for me, being there for him was worth it. Things weren't looking too good for Romeo. The prosecutor had set his ass up. The public defender didn't even have his shit together, and when the jury was told to go deliberate, I knew what was going to happen. They made my boy look like a straight-up animal. According to the prosecutor, Romeo was a big threat to society and had taken it upon himself to end two citizens' lives. "How many more of us will have to die?" the prosecutor had asked, and that in itself closed his case. It was a shame, too, and being in the courtroom made my flesh crawl. With the exception of me, all of the people were white, and they sat there waiting to get their so-called justice.

I never, ever wanted to be in Romeo's shoes, and I hated like hell that my partna was going out like this. The thought brought tears to my eyes, and I went to the bathroom to get myself together. I sat on one of the toilets, praying to God for Romeo to be set free. "Yeah, he made some mistakes," I said, looking up to the sky. "But I promise you that we both will go to church every Sunday for the rest of our lives. Please," I begged to God. "Let Romeo be found not guilty. Make a way out of no way, and all of this stuff we've been doin' will cease."

Minutes later, I went back into the courtroom, but according to public defender, the jury needed more time.

The white folks in the room looked to be in a panic, so, to me, that seemed like good news. The verdict wasn't coming back today, so I left the courthouse feeling a whole lot better. I kept thanking God for answering my prayer. Feeling upbeat, I drove to Ms. Macklin's apartment. She was already home from work, and when she opened the door, she pulled me into her arms.

"Damn, I didn't expect you to be this excited to see me," I said.

She pulled away from me and looked into my eyes. "Did . . . didn't you go to court today?"

I removed my jacket and tossed it onto her couch. "Yes, but the jury didn't have a verdict yet. I think Romeo may get out of this shit, because they put it off until another day or two."

Ms. Macklin continued to stare at me, slowly moving her head from side to side. "No, Prince. I'm sorry, but the news just reported that he was found guilty. They showed a picture of him and everything."

I rushed away from her and went into the kitchen. "I know what the fuck his public defender said. What channel was that shit on? I don't believe it."

Ms. Macklin had left the TV on the channel she was watching. When they did a recap on the news, there it was, plain as day. Romeo had been found guilty, and the prosecutor was very pleased by the verdict. I dropped back in the chair, rubbing my face hard with my hands. All kinds of emotions were running through me, and my stomach kept twisting and turning in knots. I hated life right about now, and every damn thing about it! Romeo didn't deserve that shit. How in the hell could something like this happen? I wanted to cry so badly, but I was holding my emotions in, feeling as if I was about to bust wide open. I felt vomit rush to my mouth, and that's when I swallowed. Ms. Macklin saw the pressure, and that's when she came over to me and rubbed my back.

"It's okay, Prince," she softly said. "Let it out, baby. Go ahead and let it out. At the end of the day, you, as well as Romeo, will recover from this. You're soldiers, remember? Soldiers from the hood who will make it through your trials and tribulations."

I moved my hands away from my face and looked at her with strained red eyes. Tears rushed up to them, and I couldn't hold my hurt in any longer. I tightened my fists, and as I pounded my legs, I screamed out loud.

"I hate this shit!" I blurted out in tears, rocking back and forth in my chair. "Why in the hell must life be so fucked up! And every damn time I call on God to do somethin' for me, He never listens to me! If I was white He'd listen! To hell with me, right? To hell with Romeo. What in the hell did either of us ever do to deserve this shitty-ass, poverty-stricken life!"

Ms. Macklin kneeled in front of me and held my hands. Gobs of snot dripped from my nose and ran over my lips. "Prince, I'm so sorry about this. But don't blame God. He will work this out for you, I know He will. Sometimes things happen, and we just don't understand why. We've all been through some things, and there is always a reason. You can't go around living your life with a chip on your shoulder. Be grateful . . ."

I tuned out Ms. Macklin because she just didn't understand. Nobody was looking out for me. After all that I'd been through, how long did I have to wait for God to show a nigga some direction? I was eighteen years old, and for as long as I could remember, my life had been nothing but a struggle. Struggle for love, food, money, clothes, and even fucking peace. Nothing in my life came easy, not even having a decent mother and father. Romeo's life had been the same, and as I thought about what he was feeling right now, I let out more tears. People in society were expecting too damn much from brothas like us. I figured, from now on, fuck everybody. I didn't give a damn anymore, and to hell with this so-called thing called *life!*

Ms. Macklin did her best to comfort me, but even her touch made me ill. I moved her hands away from my face and stood up to leave.

"Prince, please," she said, trying to calm me. "Don't leave under these conditions. Just chill and I'll—"

I ignored her and zipped my jacket. I smacked away the tears that continued to rush from my eyes. Damn, I hated for anyone to see me like this. I couldn't stand to look at Ms. Macklin. She did her best to convince me to stay, but to no avail. I shot out of her front door, embarrassed by my actions.

That night, I lay in my room in the dark, tossing my football in the air. What a messed-up day. Just to be sure, I watched a different channel for the ten o'clock news. They reported the same thing, and said Romeo's sentencing would be in one week. I didn't feel good about that either. The phone had been ringing off the hook, but I hadn't answered or even looked to see who it was. Thing was, I knew it wasn't Romeo, especially at no 11:30 PM I ignored the phone, and a few minutes later, my mama busted into my room fussing about the phone.

"I am so sick and tired of that goddamn phone! Please tell them bitches to stop callin' my house, or if not, I'm gettin' this number changed."

I had no response, and kept tossing my ball in the air.

"Did you hear what I said? And you need to get up and clean up this junky-ass room. I gotta step over shit just to go from one corner to another. This don't make no sense. Your lazy ass need to do somethin' around here. Why don't you get up and go clean the dishes. They've been in there for almost a week and you ain't done nothin'!"

I was in a daze and continued to ignore her. For her sake, I hoped like hell she left my room—quickly.

When Mama ordered me to get up to clean the dishes, I told her, "No. I'm not cleanin' nothin'. I ain't ate shit in this house. I suggest you wake up Raylo and ask him to do them. If not, then do them yourself."

She gritted her teeth. "I told you to get up and do them. You got ten seconds to do as you're told, and if not," she said, rolling up her sleeves, "it's you and me, baby. Right here and right now."

I could tell Mama was high, so I ignored her. I threw my hand back at her and she stepped up to my bed. She snatched my ball from me, and had the nerve to throw it at my face. I didn't even want to go there with her, but I had to. I jumped up from my bed, shoving her away from me. She stumbled backward and fell into my lamp. I left my room to get away from her, but she charged after me fists first. She pounded my back with her fists, and even though the shit didn't hurt, the fact that she was doing it pissed me off. I turned around, shoving her again. This time, she fell hard on the floor. She yelled for Raylo, and he rushed to the bedroom door, trying to see what was happening.

"Get that fool," she said, struggling to get off the floor. "He put his hands on me, baby, and I'm not gon' stand for his disrespect."

Raylo looked at me standing by the kitchen doorway. "What's up with you, fool? I know you didn't put your hands on yo' mama, did you?"

I ignored him too, and went into the kitchen to get some water. Mama came in the kitchen first, then Raylo followed. She got a butcher knife from the drawer and held it in her hand.

I looked at the knife, then guzzled down some water from the pitcher. "You'd better put that thing away, and if you aim it in my direction, you'd better use it."

Raylo saw the devious look in my eyes, and he had sense enough to try to calm the situation. "Shante, put the knife down, baby. Leave that nigga alone and come on back to bed."

I put the pitcher back into the fridge, and as I made my way to the doorway, Raylo moved aside. Mama, however, charged after me again. I wasn't sure if she had the knife in her hand, but I quickly turned around, landing a hard blow to her chest. She fell backward and skidded across the floor. The knife dropped to the ground, and she started screaming and hollering like I had killed her. Raylo grabbed me by my neck and slammed me into the wall. He flicked open a blade, and pressed it against my cheek.

"Hold it down, young blood. That there is yo' mama, and you don't do no shit like that. You feelin' like a man now or somethin'? Remember, a man can get his ass kicked too."

I eyeballed Raylo with fury in my eyes. I wasn't sure if he was going to use the blade, until he loosened his grip. He went into the kitchen to help Mama off the floor. I was starting to get that feeling again like the one I'd had earlier at Ms. Macklin's house. I wanted to scream, cry, and die, all at the same time. With my head hanging low, I went to my room and closed the door. I could hear Mama yelling and screaming about me getting out of her house, and when she busted through the door, she ordered me out.

"Get out!" she yelled. "I don't care where you go, but you will not stay another night in this fuckin' house!"

Right about now, I could have killed somebody. And before I could put my hands on Mama again, I gathered a few things in my room and left. I didn't feel like talking or being bothered by anyone, so I drove Romeo's car to an almost filled parking lot downtown and parked it. I sat thinking about all that had happened today, and I leaned over on the front seat of the car. For some reason, I got a visualization of Romeo lying on his bed in jail, doing the same thing, tears rolling down his eyes like mine, feeling as if the world was about to cave in.

A few weeks later, the world did more than cave in, it sunk in. Romeo was sentenced to thirty years, without the possibility of parole. The judge wanted to make an example out of him: hanging with the wrong crowd or not, your ass was going down! I had no way of getting in touch with him, and after what had happened between me and Mama, I wasn't going back to her house anytime soon. I had spent several nights sleeping in Romeo's car, and a few nights at Cedric's house. I hadn't seen Ms. Macklin since the day I left her apartment, and I hadn't been back to school, either. As far as I was concerned, I was now classified as a dropout. School served no purpose. Just what in the hell was a high school diploma going to get me?

Each day, I did what I felt was necessary. I stole shit, I robbed people, and I fought any nigga who looked at me too hard. I didn't give a care about nothing, and maybe being behind bars like Romeo would put me at ease. I thought about possibly doing something horrific to get myself locked up as I sat in a chair in Cedric's room, getting high as ever. We passed the joint back and forth, talking about what I needed to do in order to become a member of the gang he belonged to.

"All you gotta do is take a nigga out. You already done that shit, but I mean take out somebody who make niggas feel like, damn, that fool is *crazy*. You'll earn your respect and the fellas I roll with will have your back forever. Man, it's because of them why I'm hooked up like I am. I don't want for nothing, and anything I want, they get for me."

"Why you ain't got no car then? You got me drivin' you from point A to B in Romeo's car, yet you talkin' 'bout all this shit they do for you."

Cedric giggled. He looked like Snoop Dogg when I was messed up, but when I wasn't, he seriously reminded me of Nelly. No resemblances, but the joint we'd been hitting was fire! We were spaced out, talking shit but making no sense.

"If I wanted a car, I'd get me a car. The kind I want gotta be right, and in two or three mo' months you gon' see me rollin' like, *damn*," Cedric said, steering his hand as if a car was in front of him.

"So . . . so all I got to do is take out somebody important, right? Then they hook me up and treat me like I belong to an organization or some shit like that. I really don't need to belong to shit right about now, but . . . but, I sure do feel like hurtin' somebody."

Cedric got up and went into his closet. He pulled out a silver and black P22 silencer and laid it on my lap. "G'on and try this bad boy out. That mutha gets the job done, and you'll gain nothin' but respect with somethin' like that."

I picked up the silencer to examine it. It was heavy, but pretty as ever. I rubbed my fingers along the side of it and kissed it. I wanted to see somebody go down tonight, but the question was who. I had a long list of people on my shit list, but one person in particular came to mind.

"Let's go," I said to Cedric. "I gotta go take care of somethin'."

I tucked the silencer in the front of my pants, and took a long drag from the joint before leaving.

A half hour later, Cedric and I sat in Romeo's car, waiting for the chosen one to show up. I didn't know if he was out with one of his bitches tonight, or if he was at the pool hall with some of his friends. Maybe he was at the strip club watching the women shake their asses. Just as I ran out of assumptions, I watched him pull in his driveway. Two cars were behind him, and when I saw all three men get out, that's when I looked over at Cedric.

"Watch my back," I said. "If anybody look like they want to jump, you know what to do."

Cedric nodded and cocked his gun. Before the men went inside, I hurried out of the car and jogged across the street. My black hoodie was over my head. Dressed in all black, Derrick didn't even see me coming. I whispered his name, and that's when his head snapped to the side.

I wasted no time pulling the gun from my pants, aiming it at him. "Good night, muthafucka. Sleep tight." The silencer fired off two shots that were quiet as a mouse, but powerful. All Derrick's partnas saw was his body drop to the hard concrete, but before they could pull out their guns, Cedric dropped one of the men from a distance. The other stood with his hands held up high, away from his body. He stood stunned and shaken, not knowing what to say.

I removed the hoodie from my head. "Do you know who I am?" I asked.

He squinted and slowly nodded. "You Derrick's son, ain't you?"

I was trigger-happy tonight, and he had the wrong answer. "Wrong answer. I'm nobody you should know."

I was getting ready to unload on his ass, but he begged me not to. "You're right. I . . . I don't know you and I've never seen you before in my life. Let me live, man, and I swear there won't be no beef between us."

"Nigga, I don't trust you. You—"

"But you can," he rushed to say. "You can trust me. I'll give you anything you want and nobody will ever know what happened here."

"What I want is what's due to me. Eighteen years of back pay, and the sooner you figure out what that is, the better off you'll be."

Cedric walked up to me. "Man, why you out here negotiatin' with this fool? Kill his ass and let's go."

"No," the man said in a shaky voice. "I can take care of that for you. Just give me until tomorrow and you'll be set for life."

I told Cedric to hold his gun steady on the man and asked Cedric for his cell phone. He gave it to me, then lifted his gun where the red razor light was aimed at the man's forehead. I gave the man my gun and told him to shoot Derrick again.

"Why?" he asked.

"Evidence. If you cross me, I'll have proof that you did this, not me."

The man hesitated, but shot off two more bullets that tore holes into Derrick's chest. I took my pictures, and the man quickly handed the gun back to me.

Cedric lowered his gun, unclear about what I was doing.

"Meet me downtown tomorrow by the riverboats at noon. Have my money and you never have to see my face again," I said.

The man nodded, and Cedric and I ran to get into the car. I sped off.

He couldn't wait to ask, "That cat Derrick was yo' old dude?"

I nodded, feeling not an ounce of lost love for him.

"*Damn.* I thought I was ruthless, but you did that shit with no remorse. From what I know, he got a lot of connections, Prince. I hope that shit don't come back to haunt you."

I shrugged, not really giving a care, but hoping that his friend wouldn't cross me.

The next day, I waited downtown for Derrick's friend to show up. Surprisingly, he came. He parked right next to me, and waved for me to get into the car with him. I did, but just to be on the safe side, my silencer was right on my lap.

"Tone it down," he said, gazing at the silencer as I sat beside him with a cautious look on my face. "It's a done deal, and I promise you that as long as you keep your mouth shut, nobody will ever know what happened. To be honest, you kind of did me a favor. Derrick was gettin' a bit out of control and he couldn't be reckoned with. I was to be the next man in charge, so that's what's up."

"So, what about all the niggas he know? I heard they may come after me, but to be honest with you, I don't mind shakin', rattlin', nor rollin'.'"

"Someday, or someway . . . Maybe some shit will slip through the cracks. I'm not sayin' nothin', and since I'll be runnin' things, I'd say you have nothin' to worry about. If you want complete peace, though, I recommend takin' this money and gettin' the hell out of town. This much money brangs trouble to a nigga, and I don't know if you can handle a lot of heat comin' at you."

"How much money is it? You ain't gave me shit yet."

I was thinking about the fifty dollars Derrick had given me that day, hyping me up like it was more. I felt the same thing was about to go down, but when Derrick's partna reached for a silver briefcase on the backseat and opened it, I saw that nah, this was no game. The briefcase was filled to capacity with one hundred, fifty, and twenty dollar bills stacked high. I had never seen so much money in my life, and I couldn't believe that this shit was coming my way. I kept my eyes on the money, and could barely open my mouth to speak.

"How . . . how much is it?" I asked.

"Three hundred Gs. Now, I won't be fillin' this case up again, so spend your money wisely. Word is you're a li'l soldier. You need to keep on your mission. Trust no niggas, minimize your time on the streets, only go to war when you have to, and do right by yo' muthafuckin' kids. You'd be surprised to know how quickly money can get away from you, especially if you don't do the right things with it. Like I said, I suggest makin' a move elsewhere. I dumped Derrick's body last night, and it's gon' be just a matter of time when the shit hits the fan. Everybody gon' be talkin', and without me knowin' it, your name may or may not surface. Not sure, but just be on the safe side."

I nodded, not really understanding why this man seemed so cool with me. His advice made sense. Every fool out here claiming to be a street soldier wasn't. From listening to him, I could tell it was important for him to be on top. I guess I really had done him a favor, and now he was trying to return it. He handed the case over to me and smiled.

"Remember, I don't know you and you don't know me. Good luck, Prince Perkins, and go do you."

I got out of the car and the man sped off. I was nervous about having this much money in my possession, and the first place I went was to Cedric's house. It was a late Saturday afternoon and he was still in bed asleep. His mother told me to go into his room and wake him up.

"Wake up," I said, shaking his leg. "We got some things to do."

Cedric pulled the covers over his head and griped about getting up. I laid the suitcase on the bed, flipping it open.

"Man, you should see all this money I got. Old boy came through for me. He came through for me in a big-ass way."

Cedric pulled the covers back, and when he got of glimpse of my stacks, he quickly jumped up from his sleep.

"*Damn,*" he said with a wide grin on his face. "Where . . . How much did he give you?"

I held up three fingers. "Hundred Gs."

"Hell, naw! You hit the muthafuckin' jackpot, didn't you?"

I agreed and sat on Cedric's bed counting one stack of the money. In that stack alone there was $10,000. I tossed it to Cedric and his grin got wider. He threw the covers on the floor and hurried out of bed to put on some clothes.

That afternoon was busy. Of course, I went to the mall and hooked myself up with tennis shoes, clothes, watches, etc. I wasn't big on too much flashy jewelry, but just for the hell of it, I did buy that platinum necklace I'd seen in the window at the pawn shop. Cedric and I ate good at a steak and shrimp shack, then we drove around looking for a car for him. I already had Romeo's car, and there was no way I was getting rid of it. I planned to have it repainted, and definitely put some new wheels on it. It needed a new muffler, and some work under the hood was needed as well.

By the end of the day, Cedric had found himself a dark blue used Cadillac that needed a little work. The body looked cool, but the leather seats in the interior needed to be redone. The salesman wanted nine Gs for it, but for Cedric, it was worth it. He was hyped, and it felt good to assist a friend who had done so much for me. I told him I had a few more errands to run, and we parted ways. I wanted to see if Romeo had written me any letters, or if he'd called the house for me. Earlier today I'd finally gotten a cell phone, so I went to Mama's house to see if she would give Romeo my number. I stood before her as she sat on the couch ignoring me and watching TV.

"No, he hasn't called," she said, looking around me.

"Has he written me any letters?"

"Nope."

"I don't believe you."

Her eyes finally shifted to me. They were cold as ever. "First you put your goddamn hands on me, and now you stand there and call me a liar? What has gotten into you, Prince? You are not welcome here, and I want you out of my face, now!"

I inched my way back to the busted-up leather beige recliner and took a seat. This time, I wasn't leaving. "Look, I know I said and did some things that I shouldn't have, and what can I say other than sorry? My bad, but you've been on some mad shit too, ma. I get tired of hearin' you bitch at me all the time. Whatever happened to you bein' nice? You be treatin' me like I ain't nothin' sometimes, and how you gon' try to come at me with a knife? You could have killed me, and what? I'm supposed to stand there and let you? Nah, it wasn't going down like that."

"Fool, you know I wasn't gon' do nothin' with that knife. That's just your excuse. I will never forgive you for what you did. I don't care how bad it gets around here, I am the one person you never do that shit to. The Bible says, 'Honor thy mother and father,' Prince, so you could go to hell for what you did to me."

"Okay, that's fair. But remember, it also says, 'Do not exasperate your children; instead bring them up in the training and instructions of the Lord. For if you train a child in the way he should go, when he is old he will not run from it.' I'm your gift from God too. Are you satisfied with how you've taken care of His present to you?"

Mama threw her hand back at me. She definitely wasn't trying to hear that. "I'm very satisfied," she said.

"Then I'd say you're in denial."

She got defensive. "Look, if it wasn't for me, you wouldn't even be standin' here today, talkin' this bull. I did my best with you, Prince. I took you to church when you were little, and I gave you all kinds of books to read. I kept clothes on your back, and food in your mouth. Damn, what more do you want? This is all about you takin' responsibility for yourself. You are grown, and you need to stop sittin' back and waitin' for people to do shit for you."

"I give it to you for buyin' me books to read, but, Mama, let's be real. You took me to church two, maybe three times when I was little. The reason I know some things in the Bible is because, sometimes, I read it. That's when I ain't got nothin' else to read, but I have read some of it. I ain't no dummy, and, for as long as I can remember, I've been takin' care of myself. We can sit here and debate this forever, but you gotta admit to comin' up short on your end too."

Mama cut her eyes at me, then picked up a cigarette to light it. She took a puff, then pointed at me with the lit cigarette in her hand. "You've had it good, Prince. I don't know what the hell you keep complainin' about. Now, I could have always been a better mother, and, yes, I've made *some* mistakes. But I will not apologize to you for them. Parents are not perfect and kids need to know their place. You've had a roof over your head, and I've never left you out there on the streets. Be thankful for what you have and stop expectin' me to give you the world."

As far as I was concerned, this conversation was over. I had to accept that this was just how the relationship between me and my mama was going to be. I had gotten pretty darn used to it, but it sure would have been nice if she would have recognized her mistakes and apologized for them. I headed back to my room, just to gather some more things so I could go find a studio apartment to live in. Nothing fancy, just a place where I could lay my head down in peace and think about my plans.

I left my room with a huge duffle bag on my shoulder. By the time I got to the living room, Raylo was coming through the door with two brown paper bags in his hand. One bag looked to be wrapped around a bottle of liquor and the other bag had the aroma of Chinese food coming from it. He set the bags on the living room table, staring at me, then at Mama.

He coughed, then cleared the mucus from his throat. "I . . . I have some bad news for y'all. Prince, I'm glad you're here." Raylo pointed to the chair in the living room. "Go over there and sit down."

I wasn't sure what was up, but I took a seat in the chair. Mama looked confused too, and her face was twisted up.

"I got word today that Prince's father, Derrick, was killed. They found his body wrapped in plastic behind that grocery store over there on Fifth Street."

Raylo waited for a response. I stood up. Mama pursed her lips and I bent down to kiss her cheek. She turned it up to me.

"I'll call to give you my new address," I said. "In the meantime, here's my cell phone number. If Romeo calls, give it to him for me, please."

Mama took the piece of paper with my number on it. "All right. But you don't have to leave if you don't want to. G'on back in your room and put up your things."

"Nah, like you said, I need to start takin' care of my responsibilities. I'm good and you know I ain't gon' be no stranger."

She smiled, and stood to give me a hug.

"Damn," Raylo blurted out. "Did anybody hear what I just said?"

Mama placed her hand on her hip. "Who gives a damn? What we supposed to do? Sit up here and cry? I don't think so. You won't get any damn tears out of me."

"Exactly," was all I could say.

Raylo looked at us in awe. "Y'all some cold mutha-fuckas around here. Damn!"

I chuckled and tossed my bag over my back like a moving soldier. I was ready to be on my own, but skeptical about tackling this so-called thing referred to as life.

Chapter 13

I had gotten settled in my new studio apartment, which was above a Laundromat and soul food restaurant that lit up the whole block near South Kings highway. The apartment was just a spacious open area, where I could easily travel from one room to the next. I had very little furniture: a sofa sleeper, a two-seat kitchen set, a shelf for my books, a computer, and a plasma TV that sat on an entertainment center. By no means was it anything to brag about, but it was mine. I didn't have to worry about hearing Mama's mouth, and not having a phone that rang throughout the day and night gave me peace. I spent a lot of time playing my Xbox and PS3, and I had gotten a Wii to play too. That thing in itself kept me busy, and so did my weight bench. I was dedicated to keeping my body in shape, and since I wasn't going to school anymore, I had to do something.

A part of me really missed going to school, even more so I missed seeing Ms. Macklin. It had been at least a month since I'd seen her, and pussy had definitely been on my mind. I had been so busy, though, and for a short time, she had to be put on the back burner. I figured she was wondering where I was, so around 8:00 PM that night I put on my fresh new gear and drove to her apartment. It was still chilly outside, so I wore my short leather jacket and flipped the hood over my head.

I knocked on Ms. Macklin's door, but there was no answer. I knocked harder, but still no one came. I leaned over and peeked through her partially open blinds, but could see no one inside. It was a Tuesday, so I figured she was probably at the strip club tonight. I couldn't remember how to get there if I tried, but as soon as I turned to walk away, I heard her ask who was knocking. I placed my finger over the peephole so she wouldn't see.

"Who is it?" she asked again.

I didn't say a word, and that's when she slightly cracked the door. She looked at me through the crack and asked what I wanted.

"I came here to see you," I said. "Open the door."

She opened the door, and when I stepped inside, I saw that she had a towel wrapped around her body and one around her head.

"I take it you were in the shower," I said.

She stood by the door, holding the towel close to her chest. "Prince, where have you been? I've been worried sick about you. How dare you make me worry like this? You haven't been to school, you haven't stopped by, nothing. I thought you'd done something stupid to yourself, and when you left here that day . . ."

"I just needed to lay low for a while. As for school, sorry, but it ain't for me. I know how you feel about it, but I don't have the mindset to be there."

Ms. Macklin sadly shook her head. "How could you say that? An education is so important. You will not get ahead without it."

"We'll see," I said, taking off my jacket. "But I didn't come here to talk about school. Maybe later, but definitely not now."

I walked up to Ms. Macklin, but she held up her hand to stop me.

"I'm on my way to work tonight. Come back later this week, and be prepared to talk to me about why you feel an education isn't important."

"I never said it wasn't important. All I said is school wasn't for me. As for you goin' to work tonight, you can scratch that shit."

She took a few steps away from me. "Sorry, but I have to go make my money. Bills have to be paid, and my mother is counting on me."

"How much do you make in one night?"

"It varies. Why?"

"'Cause I want to know. Besides, doin' that shit doesn't suit you at all."

"It's not like I'm overly thrilled about it either, but where else can I make three to five grand a night?"

I reached into my jacket, pulling out a wad of money. Once I counted out five Gs, I dropped it on the living room table.

"There. Paid in full."

Ms. Macklin looked at the money with no smile on her face. "Prince, I knew you would choose that path. Selling drugs is a guaranteed jail sentence. Why would you want to end up like Romeo? I thought you—"

I sighed, in no mood to hear her lecture. "I'm not sellin' drugs. I swear to you that's not what I'm doin'."

"Then where did you get that money from?"

"Someone owed it to me. I did him a huge favor and he paid me well for doin' it."

Her eyes bugged. "Did you kill somebody? I hope you didn't kill—"

"No, nothing like that either," I lied. "I was asked to do some investigative shit for someone, and he paid me for doin' it. You gotta trust me on this, and from what you know about me, you know I ain't ever been the kind of nigga on no corner slingin' dope. This was all about helpin' somebody out. I can't get into any more details because I promised him that it would be our secret. You already know how good I am at keepin' secrets."

Ms. Macklin was reluctant to believe me. "I hope you're not lying to me, Prince. I'm not sure about this."

"No matter what, money is money, ma, and I just paid to be with you tonight. Are you up to takin' care of me, or would you prefer that I pack it up and go?"

Money could always make people see things in a different light, and Ms. Macklin was no different. The kiss I'd been waiting for finally arrived, and, rushing to get at me, she peeled off my shirt. She squatted down and pulled my jeans and boxers to my ankles. Giving me nothing but pleasure with her mouth, I stood with my eyes closed. I pumped her mouth and held her head steady as she delivered an immaculate performance. It didn't take long for my legs to weaken, and the fear of them buckling underneath me made me request that she stop. I backed away from her and we resumed our festivities on the couch. She poured her legs over my shoulders, and as I rubbed my thick head against her slit to moisten it, she stopped me.

"A condom," she said. "I have to go get a condom."

"Not right now," I said, already guiding myself inside of her. "I won't cum inside of you. I'll pull out."

"What about—"

"I ain't been havin' sex with nobody. I'm good, so don't worry. No STDs."

She complained, but I was already inside of her juicy, heated pocket. It was soaking wet, and I skillfully stroked her, slapping my thighs against her fat ass. I made sure she felt every inch of my throbbing meat. Her mouth stayed open, sucking in air and spewing dirty words that made me fuck her harder. She demanded that I have her my way, and for the next hour or so, I treated her like a rag doll, turning her from one position to the next.

Afterward, I was spent and so was she. We lay sprawled out in her bed, naked and sharing a joint.

"I know you don't want to talk about this, but I really, really miss seeing you at school. I wish you would come back. Can't you at least do it for me?"

"No. I'm not comin' back, so drop it."

I laid the joint in an ashtray and lightly ran my hands down her smooth backside. We lay silent for a while, but her head popped up when she heard the doorbell ring.

"Stay here," she said, rushing out of her bedroom and making her way to the front door.

A few minutes later, I heard a man's voice talking. As the pitch got louder, the voice sounded very familiar to me. It was Coach Johnson's voice, and when it got closer to the bedroom, I slowly sat up and rested my back against the headboard. I didn't bother to put on any clothes, as he obviously knew I was there. He appeared in the doorway, with Ms. Macklin pushing him back, asking him to leave.

I smirked at him, then reached for the joint to take a hit.

Coach Johnson moved Ms. Macklin away from the door and entered the room. "You're a sorry muthafucka," he spat. "And if you think this shit is over, you are sadly mistaken. For the life of me"—he looked at Ms. Macklin—"I cannot believe you're that damn desperate to open your legs up to somebody like him. What . . . what in the hell is wrong with you, Patrice?"

"Go," she ordered. "Don't make me have to call the police. You can't show up like this without calling."

"Since when?" he shouted. "Since you started fucking him? Give me a break. After everything that I do for you, this is how you treat me?"

"You do nothing for me, certainly not more than what you do for your wife. Go home to her, like you always do, and stop coming over here demanding things from me and trying to run my life."

Coach Johnson turned his anger to me again. "If you think, for one minute, that she ain't still throwing that pussy at me, then you're crazy. This woman loves me. Where you lie tonight, I'll be lying tomorrow. As a matter of fact, it was just, what, two days ago that I claimed your spot. Don't let the smooth taste fool you. You will, no doubt, see me again."

I got out of bed and started to put on my clothes. This was too much bullshit for me, and I couldn't care less about Ms. Macklin's relationship with Coach Johnson. I was getting what I wanted, and there was nothing but a sex thing going on between us.

"No need to hurry," I said to Coach Johnson. "I'm leaving, and you can stay here and argue with her all night for all I care. I ain't got no beef with you, nigga, but if you keep on threatenin' me and talkin' that shit, maybe I will."

I left the bedroom, passing by Coach Johnson and Ms. Macklin as they stood by the door. She followed me into the living room to get my shirt, and on my way out she kissed my cheek.

"We'll talk soon," she said.

I pursed my lips, not really caring when her version of "soon" would be. I couldn't be swooned over no pussy; it was coming at me a dime a dozen. I never had that urge in me to fight over it, and the fight in Coach Johnson's office that day was because that fool had put his hands on me first. If he didn't back off, though, I

was gon' get after his ass real soon. As for Ms. Macklin,
she was now labeled like all of the rest of the females in
my life. Without saying it, my thoughts of her weren't
good.

For three days, I sat around in my cramped studio
doing the norm: watching TV, playing video games,
lifting weights, flipping through porn magazines, reading, and spending hours on the Internet. I had wanted
to stop by Mama's house to check on her, but I wasn't
feeling up to it. When my cell phone rang, though, I
thought it was her. Instead, I got the shock of my life
when I heard Romeo's voice.

"What in the hell is up?" I smiled.

"Same ol', same ol'," he laughed. "Just takin' it day
by day. It's slow motion up in here, but what can I do?
Gotta make the best of my situation, you know?"

"I feel you, but why you ain't been tryin' to get at a
nigga?"

"Are you crazy? I've been writin' yo' ass, but the letters came back to me. Finally, your mama answered
the phone and gave me this number so I could reach
you. I thought yo' ass skipped town or somethin'."

"Nah, nothin' like that. But when I found out what
had happened, I just wanted to hurt somebody. I can't
believe it went down like that, and how . . . how you feel
about thirty muthafuckin' years?"

"Elated!" he laughed. "Hell, naw, nigga, I feel like shit.
But what can I do but do my time and someday look forward to gettin' the hell out of here."

"I'm surprised to hear you say that. You soundin' all
giddy and shit, but I know this shit ain't really sittin'
right with you."

"No, it ain't. And some days I'm up, but many days I'm down. I try not to let it get to me, but like I said, what can I do?"

"I guess you're right, but, I mean, how is it? I can't even see you bein' in there. What location . . ."

"They sent my ass to a correctional facility in Bonne Terre, Missouri. I'm sure I'll be transferred to another facility soon. Man, they really see me as a threat, but we know better, don't we? Other than that, it's awful. Beds are hard as hell, it's always dry and musty in my cell, the food ain't worth a damn, niggas always trying to punk me, and my sly-ass roomy be drivin' me crazy. I got so much shit to tell you, but I'm gon' write you, a'ight?"

"I got so much to tell you too. You ain't gon' believe all the shit that done happened. I need to hook you up with some money, so let me know where I can send it to."

"Money and books. I be bored as hell. I even started writing a story of my own. You gon' like this shit, too. It's all about soldiers like you and me."

"I can't wait to read it. And if anybody got a story to tell, it's brothas like us, ain't it? We've definitely been through some shit to write about."

"Hell, yeah!" he laughed. "Also, I wanted to tell you that I found out about my grandmother. I understand why you didn't tell me, but, man, you should have come clean."

"I wanted to, but you was already goin' through a lot. Who told you about her, your uncle?"

"Yeah, he came to see me before they sent me away. My grandmother left me a bunch of shit in her will, but too bad I can't get at it. Guess I gotta wait until I get out, but the days are tickin' away," he joked.

I rubbed my head, feeling good about speaking to him, but sad that it was under these conditions. We talked for a while longer, and I gave Romeo my new address so he could write me. I was okay after talking to him, and when I ended my call with him, I called Cedric to see what he was up to. He said he and some of his friends were at the YMCA shooting hoops, and I told him I was on my way.

Before going to the YMCA, I drove around, showing off Romeo's car that I'd had repainted the same color. The radio system I had hooked up was blasting Drake's latest hit, and as I cased the north side, people kept turning their heads. Some looked at me with disgust, while others bobbed their heads to my music. Yeah, I liked that shit, and when I spotted this thick-booty chick walking down the street, I sped up to check her out. As I got closer, I saw that it was Nadine. From the back, she looked pretty damn good. Her front, though, was a mess. Her belly was hanging low, her face had gotten fatter, and she looked mean as hell. She still looked like Raven-Symoné, though, and I had to admit, she was very pretty. I slowly cruised by her, and when I looked in my rearview mirror, I noticed her head hanging low. She wiped her eyes and almost tripped on something in front of her. Something inside of me wouldn't allow me to keep on driving, so I pulled my car over. When she strolled by, she turned her head and saw that it was me. I lowered my window.

"Ay, where you goin'?" I asked.

She slightly bent down and looked into the car. "Why you worried about it?"

"I'm not. I just asked."

"Home," she said, continuing to walk off.

I slowly drove next to her. "Get in and let me take you home."

Nadine hesitated, but opened the car door to get in. Instead of driving her home, I drove to Fairground Park and parked my car.

She got all antsy and started rolling her neck. "I hope you didn't bring me here to have sex with you. That ain't ever happening again, and if that's what you came here for, you can take me home."

"Never say never, but, uh, no, that's not why I brought you here. I need to say somethin' to you, but please listen before you start runnin' your mouth."

She pursed her lips, but turned to give me her attention.

I looked down at her belly. "How much longer you got?"

"Two months, why?" she snapped.

"Can you stop with the attitude?"

"As a matter of fact, I can't. Every time I see you, it just irks the hell out of me. And you know why, Prince? Do you really want to know why?"

"I already know why, but I know you're dyin' to tell me yourself."

"Because you played the shit out of me. You did me so, so wrong and left me to deal with something that I was in no way ready for. I've already quit school, and my mother and me argue almost every damn day about this baby. I am stressed out, and there are days that I just want to kill myself. You, on the other hand, are riding around all high and mighty, being with all your little girlfriends. You act like you don't have a care or worry in the world. In the meantime, I'm losing my mind. I don't know what kind of good I can bring to this baby, and, thanks to you, I have become nothing but a statistic." She paused to wipe the tears from her eyes.

"Are you done, ma?" I asked, not sure how to handle her emotions. She didn't respond, so I continued. "All I can say is that you are so wrong about me around here livin' all high and mighty. I'm dealin' with some shit too. You have no idea how severe—"

"I don't care what you're dealing with. Nothing you're going through can be more painful than what I'm going through at seventeen years old!"

"I'm not goin' to sit here and argue with you about who got the most problems. Shit, we both do, and that's obvious. All I wanted to say to you is, I don't really know if this baby is mine—"

She put her hand on the doorknob to exit. "Why do you keep saying that shit?" she screamed. "I'm tired of hearing it, Prince. You know damn well that this baby is yours."

I grabbed her arm. "Would you calm down and listen? You gon' have one fucked-up baby if yo' ass don't stop stressin' over stupid shit."

"*We* gon' have a fucked-up baby. I don't care what you say, and I don't care who else at that school is claiming to be pregnant by you, but this here baby," she said, pointing to her stomach and continuously wiping her tears, "this is yours!"

"Okay, fine. So, maybe it is. Now what, Nadine? If it's mine, then I'll deal with it when the time comes."

"Well, it's coming soon."

"Good. Now stop charging at a nigga like a pit bull, and hear what I'm sayin' to you. I think it may be mine, but if it ain't, I swear I'm goin' to hurt you for playin' games and puttin' my business out there on the street. There's just so many females out here lyin' on me, and even though I had sex with most of them, sometimes I didn't even cum. I know you were a virgin when we got together, and yo' shit was chokin' me every time I got in it. So, maybe I do believe you and I admit to possibly bein' in denial. Forgive me, a'ight?"

She rolled her eyes and cracked a tiny smile. She then lightly pushed my head to the side with her finger. "Big denial. It's good to hear you talkin' like you got some sense, and I hope your kindness lasts."

"Don't count on it, but I need you to do a couple of favors for me."

"I should have known it was something. What is it?"

I started the car, and pulled away from the curb. "First," I said, "I want you to go back to school. Ain't no need for your baby to have two damn parents without high school diplomas. Someday that shit may be too embarrassing to explain."

"Then why don't you go back to school?"

"I would, but you're much smarter than me. I choose you."

"That's not so. You're smart too, Prince, and if I have to stay at home to take care of *our* baby, then what's going to be your excuse?"

"It's this thing called life that's standin' in my way. I ain't quite figured it out yet, and I'm tryin' like a muth-afucka to get a better understandin'."

"I feel you on that, but I don't know about the school thing yet. I gotta see how all of this plays out. If I can figure out a way to do it, I will."

"Try hard. For you, it will be worth it. More so than for me."

"I disagree, but you ain't ever been one to listen to me. The way you play ball, you are bound to get a scholarship. How can you let an opportunity like that pass you by?"

"I used to be passionate about playin' ball, but not anymore. Like I said, and I won't say it again, school is a closed chapter in my life."

Nadine sat silently. When we got to her house, I reached underneath the seat and pulled out a black plastic bag. I counted out $7,000 and laid it on her lap.

"That's one grand for every month that you've been pregnant. Get some things for your baby."

Her eyes were stuck on the money and she flipped through it. "Is this real? And it's our baby, not just mine."

"Okay, then our baby. I don't know if or when I'll be able to kick you out anything else, and it's all I can do for right now. Besides, I'm still not one hundred per-cent sure about bein' the father, and—"

Nadine covered my mouth. "Yes, you are, so stop say-ing it. You'll have proof when he's born, and I want a sincere apology when you have to admit to him being one hundred percent yours."

"And you'll get it."

Nadine took the money from her lap and put it into her purse. "Where did you get this from? Are you sell-ing drugs?"

"Why every time somebody around here got some money, they gotta be sellin' drugs?"

"'Cause that's how it is around here. Now, if you want me to pretend otherwise, I can."

"I got a job doin' some investigative work and I'm paid very well for doin' it."

Nadine cut her eyes, in total disbelief of what I'd said. Still, she thanked me for the money, and looked over at me before she got out of the car.

"What is it?" I asked.

"Ain't you gon' kiss me or something? I know you want a kiss from me."

I laughed my ass off and slapped my leg. "Hell, nah, ma! It ain't goin' down like that. I ain't tryin' to hook up with yo' crazy ass again. The spit action was enough, and you can't spit on me and then try to give me some pussy."

"I can do whatever I want to do, and you shouldn't have been running around here denying our baby."

"Good-bye, Nadine. Go inside and shake off some of that madness you still talkin'."

"Are you going to take me to the mall next week so I can get some things for the baby?"

I sighed. "Look, I ain't into all of that shit. That's why I gave the money to you. For now, my participation will be minimal. Accept what I'm sayin' and run with it. Besides, I may be in one of my moods next week and don't want to be bothered."

Nadine got out of the car looking much happier than she was when I had first seen her. I was glad about that, and was serious as hell about her returning to school. I hoped she listened, as, now, her future was just as important as mine.

Chapter 14

After talking to Nadine about my son, I was starting to get a slight grip on my life. It seemed like I had something good to look forward to, and if a baby was going to change my life around, then I was all for it. Meanwhile, I felt bad about abruptly leaving Ms. Macklin's apartment that day and not calling her. Yeah, we had this sex thing going on, but I in no way wanted her to feel as if she was being used by me, even though we were using each other. When I stopped by her apartment the other night, she didn't come to the door. I knew how to get in touch with her if I wanted to, and that was by going up to the school. I glanced at my watch, and saw that fifth hour was just about ready to start. Since I no longer went to school, I wasn't sure if the security guards would let me in, but it was worth a try.

As soon as I entered North High School, the security guard stopped me at the door. He was one of the more laidback guards, so I knew I'd be able to get in.

"No can do," he said with his arms folded.

"Man, I need to go to the principal's office."

"For what?"

"I wanted to talk to Mr. King about returnin' to school. He said I could talk to him."

"Did you make an appointment?"

"Nah, but I was drivin' by and thought it would be a good idea to stop."

The security guard gave me a suspicious look, then checked me for weapons. "Go," he said. "And next time, make an appointment."

I thanked him and headed in the direction of the principal's office. The security guard watched me, too, and when I opened the door to the principal's office, the guard looked away. I quickly snuck off down the hall, and turned down another hallway. Ms. Macklin's class was only a few feet away, and when I looked through the glass panel on the door, I saw her standing at the chalkboard. She was writing on the board, with one hand on her hip. The fuchsia dress she wore hugged every curve, and I couldn't believe I was missing out. I looked at the students in the class and there was not one empty seat. I seriously thought about not going inside, and I knew if I did, all of the rumors about us would be confirmed. I no longer went to this school, so I didn't give a fuck. I was sure Ms. Macklin would know how to handle this, and thinking about how bold I could be, I finally pulled on the door. I entered the room, and every single head turned my way. Ms. Macklin's writing on the board came to a halt and she looked stunned to see me.

"Excuse me," I said to the class. "I don't mean to interrupt."

I walked up to Ms. Macklin and put my arm around her waist. She attempted to back away from me, but my grip was tight.

"I know you were at the crib when I stopped by the other night. Get at me when you can, ma, a'ight?"

I pecked her lips, and as expected, she didn't reciprocate. She knew she could get fired behind this, so she hurried to push me away. The students in the classroom were shouting out "damn's" and "dang's" to "uh-uh's" and "no, he didn'ts!" There was much laughter, too, and as I slightly stumbled backward, I dropped a piece of paper with my address and phone number on it. I backed out of the room, continuously watching the shocked look on her face.

I was happy when I left her classroom, only because I had a vision of my events for the night. I wasn't sure if the security guard was looking for me, but I also wanted to stop by Coach Johnson's office. I walked fast down the hall, then jogged down the steps to the lower level where his office was. His door was open, and when I looked inside, his head was lowered. He was looking at some papers in front of him. I knocked twice and his head went up.

"Can I come in?" I asked.

He stood up, slowly pulling off his jacket. "Sure," he said. "You want to talk again? I didn't think you'd be back so soon, especially after that last ass kicking I gave you."

Obviously, Ms. Macklin had him all fucked up. He seemed ready to kill for her, and this dude was fucking me up.

"Man, like I said before, I ain't got no beef with you. Sit down and chill," I said.

I closed his door, but Coach Johnson did not take a seat. He put his balled fists on his hips, asking why I was there.

"I had to take care of somethin', but, uh, I wanted to stop by and talk to you about some thangs."

"Speak."

"I usually don't warn people about what will happen to them if they keep up mega shit with me, but since we may be seeing each other from time to time, I wanted to encourage you to back off. I suggest you find a way to cope with me laying the pipe to your mistress, and if you don't, your wife may soon be without a husband. I'm just sayin'."

Coach Johnson smirked. "I . . . I can't believe you, Prince. How did someone like you ever get so fucked up? You was my star football player, yet you chose to drop out of school and fall in love with your teacher? Who, by the way, is deeply in love with me. I just don't get it, but when I was your age, I guess I did some stupid shit too. Nothing as bad as what you're doing, but you'll have to be the one who lives and learns from your own mistakes."

"How old are you, Coach Johnson? Thirty-eight, right? I can't believe you're that old and still confused about the meanin' of love. It makes sense, though, comin' from a man who claims to love his wife, yet disses her for a cheap thrill. FYI, Coach, I'm not in love with no one. I love to have sex with a woman who gives it to me good and knocks me off my feet. I don't have to tell you about it, for you already know how it is. But pussy ain't somethin' I feel as if I want to kill a nigga over. There's too much of it to go around, and what one female won't give, another one will. I'm wise enough to know that, and as far as football is concerned, fuck you and the game. What's meant to be will be, and there wasn't a chance in hell I would keep playin' for you to save my soul. With that, control yourself or get ready to be dealt with."

I turned to walk out the door, having nothing else to say.

He cleared his throat. "I guess you know she's pregnant, right? But then again, you wouldn't know because she's done fucking with you. No woman wants a man who doesn't stand up and fight for her, nor one who walks out when he's under pressure. Through consoling her the other night, that's how I found out she was pregnant. I doubt that the baby is mine, because I strapped up. It could be yours or anyone else, for that matter, but that is what happens when you play with fire. As for you, young man, you got a lot of fires burning. I don't know what kind of shit you shooting from your dick, but whatever it is, it's potent. Rumor has it that you have four chicks pregnant—no, three, because one of them just had her baby. Now, you may have to add Patrice to that list. What you gon' do with all these kids, Prince? Get a job and take care of them? Teach them good morals and values, make sure they get a good education, what? Nah, you ain't gon' do nothing like that. You gon' leave them babies out there on the streets, lost as fuck like you and looking for a way to survive. Sadly, that's the kind of nigga you are, and a street soldier you are not. Now, I got work to do. You can get out of my office, or I'll be happy to call security to come get you out."

I wanted so badly to fire back at him, but I don't know what stunned me more: the fact that Ms. Macklin was pregnant, or that there was possibly a child in this world who belonged to me. I put on my game face in Coach Johnson's office, but when I left, I sat in my car, thinking hard. Ms. Macklin and I only had sex twice without a condom. One time I came inside of her, but the other time I didn't. Well, I didn't think I did, but fuck! What was wrong with my ass? Every time I touched a chick she got pregnant. I really wasn't sure about being the father of nobody's baby, and Nadine's baby was the only one I really thought was mine. Everybody thought I was gon' be a big time football player, and dollar signs were flashing. Maybe now they realized that shit wasn't going to happen. Either way, I had to put some of this mess to rest. I was going to make some phone calls tonight, just to see what was up. As for Ms. Macklin's situation, all I could say about that was *damn!* Coach Johnson very well may have been trying to cover his ass because he was married. I knew he didn't want to throw no news like that on his wife, and it was easy to pin the baby on me. It was all good, though, and at the end of the day, the truth would come to the light.

I sat on my sleeper sofa that night, making my first call to a chick at my school named Deborah. Unfortunately for me, she was the one who Coach Johnson said recently had the baby. When she answered the phone, I was at a loss for words. I could hear the baby crying in the background, and I listened to Deborah say hello again.

"What's up?" I said, clearing my throat. "This Prince."

She was silent for a moment, but then spoke up. "What do you want?"

I rubbed my chest and swallowed. I couldn't believe how nervous I was speaking to her. "I heard you had your baby. People been sayin' I'm the father, so I want to know what's up."

"I thought you was, but you ain't. My baby daddy go to another school, and he here with me now. I gotta go. I'll talk to you some other time."

I released a heap of air from my mouth and sighed with relief. "Yes," I yelled, tightening my fist and shutting my phone. Two down—Nadine and Deborah—and two, maybe three more to go. I opted not to call Monesha, only because I deep down did not believe that slut was pregnant by me. I hadn't heard anything else from her or her father, so I left that situation as was. The other girl who was running off at the mouth was Ivory. I spoke to her, but she wasn't backing down. I was the father, and that's all there was to it. She was due in three months and was willing to go through with a paternity test to prove it. "Holler at me when the time comes," was all I had to say.

I felt good about getting some of those issues off my chest. By now, I'd hoped to hear from Ms. Macklin, but it was getting late. I didn't feel like being cooped up in my apartment tonight, so I called Cedric to tell him I was on my way. He asked me to meet him at a pizza joint near his house, so I made my way there.

I entered the pizza parlor, and spotted Cedric playing a pinball machine in the far corner. There were two machines, so I played the one next to his.

"I gotta ask," he said. "Did you really kiss Ms. Macklin in her classroom today? Everybody talkin' about that shit, and I can't believe you went out like that."

"Yeah, I did it. I just wanted her to know how much I'm diggin' her. I dropped my number for her to call me."

"That was some bold shit, wasn't it? I didn't know you were feelin' her like that."

"Yep," I said, keeping it short.

We continued to play the machines, and, afterward, we sat down with three chicks who went to our school and ate two large pepperoni and double sausage pizzas. All the chicks wanted to talk about was what had happened today at school with Ms. Macklin, the girls who claimed to be pregnant by me, and, of course, why me and Cedric had dropped out of school. They mentioned Romeo, too, and one of them claimed that her cousin was at the same jail facility that Romeo was at in Bonne Terre. She said that Romeo and his cellmate were lovers. I almost cursed that bitch out for lying, and it frustrated me that a rumor like that would travel so far.

After the girls left, Cedric said he was going to take a leak and would be right back. I waited for him, and then we walked outside to our cars. We talked for a while, and then he got in his car and jetted. No sooner had I opened the door to mine than a brotha dark as midnight walked up on me, asking if I had a light.

"Nah, bruh," I said, gazing into his sneaky eyes. I knew what a thief in the night looked like, but before I could open my car door, he made a move. He pulled out a shiny blade, holding it to my throat. My arm was being twisted behind my back, and the way he held it caused severe pain to shoot up my arm.

"Up your wallet and empty yo' pockets, nigga! If you make a false move, I'll cut yo' goddamn throat!"

The blade was pinching my neck, so I was careful not to trip. I reached into my pocket, then dropped my wallet on the ground. He dug in my pockets, and put the wad of money I had into his pocket. My car door was already open, so he punched me in my stomach, tearing up my gut with powerful blows. I fell to the ground, and all I could feel were the soldier marks he was delivering to my body. I could barely move, and my body was starting to feel numb. I shielded my face with my hands, but as he kept stomping me, my face and hands bounced against the concrete. Lying there helpless, I saw the nigga open my car door and check my car. The first place he looked was underneath my seat. Moments later, he came out with the bag of money I'd kept underneath there. He opened the glove compartment, and inside he found my platinum chain. I was so afraid that he'd see my silencer underneath the passenger's seat, but his head jerked up when he heard a man ask if I needed some help.

"Yes," I strained to say, with blood gushing from my mouth. The brotha jumped out of the car, and just for the hell of it, his green and white laced-up Nike shoe kicked me right in my face. I swore I heard my neck crack, but lucky for me, it didn't. All I heard were his footsteps running away. I rolled on my back, staring up at the dark sky. I had no idea how badly I was hurt, but the man rushed over to help me.

"I'm going inside to call 911. Hang in there, brotha," the man who was trying to help said.

In no way did I want the police on the scene. I had my silencer in the car, and finding that alone would send me to jail for life. I eased up, tightly gripping my midsection. Slowly making my way to my feet, I sat in my car, trying to get myself together. I could feel what my face looked like, and I used my shirt to wipe it down. A whole lot of blood covered my shirt and my face burned like hell. Not as much as my stomach was burning, but, unfortunately, I wasn't up to visiting no doctor. I had a gut feeling about this shit, a feeling that led me to Cedric's house. I parked down his street, waiting to see if he showed. His car wasn't there yet, but I knew it would soon come. I slid down in my seat, resting my head against the window. I was hurting so bad, and I hoped like hell that my suspicions didn't pan out to be true.

Almost an hour later, Cedric pulled in front of his house. He went inside, but nearly twenty minutes after that, another car pulled up. There were two niggas inside, and after the driver blew the horn, Cedric came outside. The first thing I saw when the driver stepped out of the car was his green and white Nike tennis shoes. Something horrible went through me. This was why I didn't like hanging with a bunch of fake-ass niggas. Cedric had set my ass up good, or so he thought. He was gon' pay for this shit. He and his friends sat outside for a minute, smoking a blunt and laughing. I actually saw dude describing how he stomped my ass on the ground, and he laughed hard as he must have been describing his final blow to my face. He slapped hands with Cedric, and with a cigarette dangling from ol' boy's mouth, I saw him count out some money, putting it into Cedric's hand. Afterward, Cedric put up his fist and hurried inside. The other two fellas got in the car and drove off.

Knowing exactly how much had been stolen from me, I was down to less than a hundred Gs. They took the bulk of my money, even though I hadn't been spending much at all. I should have known better than to keep my money underneath the seat. I thought it was tucked away pretty good. The rest was at home in my closet, but I really didn't feel safe with it being there. The landlord had a key to get inside whenever he wanted to, but there really was no other place that I could keep it. Mama's house was not an option, because as much as she snooped around, I was sure she would find it. For now, I intended to leave the rest of my money exactly where it was, and never again would I keep that much money on me.

Fifteen minutes had gone by, and that's when I called Cedric.

"Say, man," I said in a soft tone.

"Who dis?"

"Prince. It's Prince."

"What's up, bro?"

"After you left the pizza joint, I got robbed. Ol' boy fucked me up, Ced, and I'm at my mama's house right now. She gon' take me to the hospital, but I need you to do somethin' for me."

"I will, but are you okay? I mean, how bad are your injuries? You talkin' about goin' to the hospital and you soundin' like you on your last breath."

"I feel like it too, but, uh, that nigga got me for almost two hundred grand," I lied. "I saw him dump some of it in the Dumpster behind the pizza joint. Maybe he was hidin' it from somebody, but see if it's still there for me. I can't even move right now, and I feel like my ribs are cracked."

"Damn, Prince, that shit fucked up. I'll go check it out for you, and if it's there, you know I got you. We gon' find out who that nigga was, so don't worry about it right now. Be well and I'll get at you later about the money."

"Thanks, bruh. Thanks."

I hung up, knowing that Cedric would be leaving, thinking he'd gotten swindled by his friends. Sure enough, he left his house, flying to get to the Dumpster behind the pizza joint. I followed several car lengths behind him, and watched as he parked beside the Dumpster. His head was down, and as he was searching through the Dumpster, I started his way in my car. My bright lights were beaming, and I could see him squinting. He put his hand over his eyes to shield them from the brightness, but, by then, my silencer was already out of the window. I fired off one shot that whistled as it left my Glock, instantly dropping him. Just to be sure that he was a done deal, I slowly got out of the car, pumping more shots into his chest and busting it open. Blood splattered, and as I damn sure took care of him, it was time to see about me.

Chapter 15

As far as I knew, nobody suspected that I had anything to do with what had happened to Cedric. I was at the hospital getting bandages placed on my ribcage and stitches on the cut on my cheek that wouldn't stop bleeding. My other bruises needed time to heal, and since my swollen face made me look like a monster, I wasn't going anywhere. I stayed cooped up in my apartment for almost two weeks. The only time I left was to go dump the trash.

I had written Romeo a letter, and when I got one back from him, I sat on the sofa to read it. Like all of his letters, it was short, and he claimed to be bored as ever. I noticed that he kept talking about his roommate a lot, and in the letter I'd written to him, that prompted me to bring up what the chick at the pizza joint had said that day. Romeo responded by saying, "Fuck them bitches. I hope you don't believe that bullshit." He also wrote, "Nigga gotta do whatever to stay afloat."

I couldn't wait for him to call so I could ask what that meant, and, just my luck, the next day he called to talk.

"You said in your letter, 'a nigga gotta do whatever to stay afloat,'" I repeated. "I wasn't sure how to interpret your words."

"Man, you can take them how you want to, but is what I do up in this mutha really that important?"

"To me it is. Nigga, you supposed to be a soldier. What's up with that? I just got a real big-ass problem if you up in there doin' dudes. I . . . I don't know what to say about that shit, Romeo. I ain't never pegged you out to be like that."

"Get a grip, nigga. I told you it ain't goin' down like that. I can't believe you're lettin' a rumor fuck with yo' head. Don't you have somethin' better to talk about?"

He was too damn defensive for me, but what the hell. I had no idea what being in prison was like, so I changed the subject. We started talking about Ms. Macklin, and I spoke in codes about what I had done to Cedric. Romeo advised me not to trust anyone and we ended our call on a pretty good note. No doubt, I missed my partna like hell. At times, it felt as if life wasn't even worth living without him around.

Later that day, I drove to Mama's house to see what was up with her. As always, she was in the living room, watching TV. Raylo wasn't there, and we both sat on the couch talking while sharing a joint.

"Did you put some ice on your face to help the swellin'?" she asked, standing up over me. She moved my head from side to side, shaking her head as she observed my soldier marks. "Somebody really messed you up. I told you about runnin' them streets. Being out there ain't nothin' but trouble."

"I was out eatin' pizza and playin' video games. I can't stay cooped up forever. There are always gon' be fools out there on the street tryin' to see what they can get from the next man. Trust me, I know, as once upon a time I was one of them."

"You ain't got shit to get, with yo' broke ass. What is it that they were tryin' to get?"

Yeah, her words stung, but fuck it. I let it roll off my back. "Money. That fool wanted my money, and he got it too."

"How much?"

"About a hundred and a quarter."

Mama sat down and drank from the Grey Goose bottle in front of her. "He beat your ass like that for a hundred and twenty-five dollars? Please. These fools are crazy. You should have blown his damn brains out."

"Don't worry. It's all taken care of. And, for your information, it wasn't hundreds, it was thousands."

She cocked her head back and her eyes bugged. "Boy, quit playin'. You ain't have no hundred thousand dollars on you, did you?"

I nodded. "Yep."

"Why didn't I know you had that kind of money? And why in the hell didn't you give none of it to me? Shit, I'm livin' in this shack and you ridin' around with thousands in your damn pockets. What kind of shit is that? Boy, you are somethin' else. After all I've done for you, you should be ashamed of yourself."

"I was gon' give you some of it, but I thought you was gon' question me about where I got it. Obviously, that doesn't matter to you. Besides, I wasn't tryin' to hide it from you. How did you think I got my apartment, these clothes, the car fixed up, and my jewelry? You should have been payin' more attention."

"I haven't even seen your apartment, and that's because you haven't invited me over there. As for the other stuff, I figured yo' ass was sellin' drugs. That's what is obvious, and like I said, you'd better be careful foolin' around on those streets. If another nigga won't get ya, the police definitely will."

Mama sipped from the bottle of Grey Goose again, then handed it to me. "Nah, I'm good," I said, reaching into my pocket. I pulled out another wad of money, and laid two grand on the table. "I try not to keep a lot of money on me anymore, but you can have that. If you need somethin' else, let me know."

She picked up the money and stuffed it inside of her bra. "What kind of drugs are you sellin'?" she asked.

"I'm not sellin' drugs. You said I'm sellin' drugs, not me."

"Then where are you gettin' all this money from?"

I stood up and stretched. I knew our conversation was about to get deep, and Mama was being too nosey. "Let's just say that I got it from my sperm donor."

Mama's eyes bugged again. "Who, Derrick? I thought that fool was dead."

I leaned down and kissed Mama's cheek. "Dead as a doorknob," I whispered. "And you can pat me on my back and thank me later."

Mama jumped to her feet and stomped them. "Shut up, Prince," she shouted. "Boy, don't you tell me you . . ."

I placed my fingers on her lips. "Shh. Chill, a'ight? You lookin' too excited and I don't know what for."

She put her hand on her hip. I could tell the alcohol was brewing. "Did you kill yo' daddy?" she whispered.

"No," I said, putting on my jacket to go.

"Then, what are you talkin' about then?"

"Nothin', Mama. Maybe one day you'll figure it out, but for now, I'm out."

She playfully smacked me on the back of my head. "Come get me next week so I can see your apartment. Until then, please call that hood rat who called here claimin' she just had your baby. I told her ass I ain't tryin' to be nobody's grandma, and please do not bring that *thing* over here."

I frowned, not from hearing about the baby, but because Mama was just now telling me. "Who was it that called?"

"Shit, I can't remember. Uh, it was . . . what's-her-face. That kind of chunky one with the cute face."

"Nadine?"

"Yeah, her. Is that really yo' baby?"

I stood silently, not knowing that Nadine had already had the baby. "Why you just now tellin' me?"

"'Cause I didn't know if it was your baby. These heifers be out here playin' around with that shit too much, and on the *Maury* show they be lyin' their butts off. You'd better get a paternity test and make sure that baby belongs to you. You don't want to be takin' care of nobody else baby, and those fools on *Maury* . . ."

I tuned Mama out. The possibility of my son being here made me nervous. I wasn't sure if I was ready for this shit, and even though I wanted to call Nadine to see what was up, I couldn't do it. Besides, she'd want me to come over and my face was still messed up. I didn't want the baby to look at me and get scared. I'd wait, maybe another day, a week or two, to go see what was up.

I left Mama's house, and returned home about ten o'clock that night. As I was walking up the black steel steps, I could tell it was a woman coming down them in high-heeled shoes. I figured it was my neighbor, whose studio apartment was next to mine, but when I looked up, I saw that it was Ms. Macklin. She wore a long trench coat, and a gray pantsuit was underneath. I rarely saw her in a pair of pants, but no matter what she had on, I was glad to see her. I didn't let my enthusiasm show, and by the look on her face, she wasn't letting hers show either.

I walked up a few more steps until I was in front of her. "I didn't know you were stoppin' by. Why didn't you call? I could have gotten here sooner."

"I thought about calling, but I was in the neighborhood. I took my chances on you being here."

I walked past Ms. Macklin and she followed me to my apartment. I knew the inside was a mess, and I

started to ask her to wait by the door until I tidied up. I
didn't want to take any chances on her leaving, though,
so I went ahead and let her inside.

"You have to excuse my bachelor pad. I live here by
myself, and I don't clean up as much as I should."

Actually, when we got inside, it wasn't all that bad.
I had a few books spread out on the floor in the living
room, and an empty TV dinner tray was on the table. An
empty soda can was next to it, but the porn magazine
on the table was something I was sure she didn't care to
see. My sleeper sofa had been pushed up to a sofa, but
the sheets that I had to cover the sleeper were hanging
out. The kitchen had a pile of dishes in the sink, but the
most embarrassing was the smell of dirty socks. I told
Ms. Macklin to have a seat on the sofa, and I sprayed
several squirts of the Glade spray that was sitting in my
huge picture window, which had no curtains.

"There," I said, putting the can on the table and sitting back on the sofa. I put my arms on top of it, and
looked over at her.

She cleared her throat from the fragrance and
coughed. "Wha . . . what happened to your face?"

I was so thrilled to see her that I'd completely forgotten that my face was still bruised. "I got into a fight. As
you can see, I lost. It wasn't the first time I got soldier
marks and I'm sure it won't be the last."

"That's not good. I had hoped that you were focusing on getting yourself together, but I see that I am so
wrong about you, again."

I could tell she had attitude, but I wasn't going there
with her today. "Enough about me. What's up with you
and this baby you carryin'?"

She almost looked shocked that I knew. "Who told
you I was pregnant?"

"Your boyfriend did."

"I don't have a boyfriend."

"Then your late-night creeper did. I'm surprised he didn't tell you that he told me, especially since he's been pickin' up the pieces after me."

"Whatever Prince. Coach Johnson and I have an on-again, off-again relationship that I'm getting pretty darn tired of. He's a nice man, though, and it's hard for me to give up on him because he's married."

I definitely wasn't trying to hear about her relationship with Coach Johnson. That madness was her business. "Yeah, yeah, yeah, but, uh, you still ain't talkin' about the baby."

"There is no baby."

"What happened to it?"

She looked down, and fumbled with her nails. "I had an abortion."

I sighed a little from relief. "So, who was the father? Did you know?"

She hesitated before answering, then looked over at me. "Coach Johnson and I always used condoms. Not once did we not use one. I think the baby was yours, but I can't be sure. I had sex with no one else, and I don't care if you believe me or not."

"Why did you have an abortion then?"

Her eyes widened. "Do you really have to ask me that? You aren't ready to be no father, Prince, and I can't say that I was ready to be a mother. I have so many issues to deal with. I'm afraid that I may lose my job as a teacher if the school board finds out I'm a stripper. I don't trust Coach Johnson not to say anything, and since he's upset with me, there's no telling what he will do. Before I can even think about bringing a baby into this world, I must get my life together."

"I feel you on that, but why you just now tellin' me about this? I've been waitin' to hear from you. I know you ain't mad at me for leaving that day, or for coming up to the school, are you?"

"No. I just needed time to sort through some things. I have a lot going on, Prince, and my life is truly one big mess. We never talked much about it, but I have got to figure out a way to get myself on the right track. As for your visit to the school that day, it hasn't made my life any easier. I'm being questioned by many of the students about our relationship, and I had to send one chick to the office for calling me a slut. Mr. King called me into his office, questioning me about what you did. I had to explain that you had lost your mind. He's banned you from coming to that school, so you aren't allowed to come there anymore."

I threw my hand back. "Fuck him. You wouldn't come to your door, so I had to do what I had to do. I wasn't tryin' to sweat you, and I know where I stand with you. I'm cool with that. If you want to see other niggas, do what you gotta do. I'm just a brotha, tryin' to have fun and have fun with the lady I'm with. I ain't lookin' for a bunch of drama. You can save that mess for Coach Johnson."

She listened to my words but had no response. Instead, she picked up the porn magazine from the table and started to flip through it. "Tuh," she commented. "What the . . ." She flipped through more pages. "This is . . . You are so damn nasty." She kept looking through the magazine, then laid it on her lap. "I know it's not of any relevance to you, but I think Coach Johnson and I are just about over. He got worked up over me being pregnant, and it drove me crazy, seeing how controlling he was."

"You think I don't know that's the real reason you had an abortion? He made you do it, just in case the baby was his, didn't he?"

A blank expression fell on her face. "Are you crazy? Don't nobody make me do anything. I told you why I had an abortion, and when reality set in, I do believe that child was yours."

"Look, ma, I don't care if it was or not. I also don't care to hear anything else about you and Coach Johnson. That's your headache."

She looked down at the magazine again. Since she seemed to be all into it, I scooted over closer to her.

"Let me show you the one who reminds me of you," I said, taking the magazine from her.

"Please. Not one woman in that magazine looks like me. I'm in a category all by myself."

I chuckled and found the chick who had assets like Ms. Macklin. I pointed to the young woman's stuff in the magazine, showing it to Ms. Macklin.

"That one. That pussy right there looks just like yours."

She snatched the magazine and frowned at it "Like hell!" she yelled. "My stuff don't look nothing like that, and I can't believe you pointed to her out of all of the women in here."

"How do you know what your stuff looks like? Do you be checkin' it out in a mirror or somethin'?

"Yes. And I can see it when I look down."

"You can't see all up in it like I can. I'm tellin' you right now that your stuff looks like hers."

Ms. Macklin hit me with the magazine and I flipped through some more pages. I found the woman who had an ass that reminded me of hers and I pointed to the picture. "Now, you can't deny this ass. That is your butt, hands down."

She looked at the picture, but didn't deny that one. "Okay. You may be on to something, but the other one is a definite no."

I kissed the woman's butt in the magazine and licked her crack. "Mmm," I said. "I've been fantasizin' about this ass for a long time."

Ms. Macklin snatched the magazine away from me, and tore the page out of it. She balled up the page, and tried to toss it in a trashcan on the other side of the room. She missed.

"Ha, that's what you get," I shouted.

"Be quiet with your nasty, horny self. I'm sure that tramp got a serious workout from your lips. I'm surprised that magazine isn't all wet and sticky."

"Are you jealous? You sound real, real jealous."

"I am." She pouted and folded her arms.

I got on the floor and kneeled down in front of her. I took her hands with mine and held them. "Don't be mad. Those chicks in that magazine ain't got a damn thing on you."

Ms. Macklin lifted her hand and softly rubbed my face.

"I know," I said, allowing her to touch my face. "It's ugly, ain't it? My bruises should heal soon. I hope they don't bother you."

"No," she whispered. "I just hate that you've been through so much, that's all."

"I don't believe that looking at my face doesn't scare you," I said, reaching over to the lamp next to her and turning it off.

The room was pitch black, and she touched my face again.

"I see beyond the outside of your face, and I hope you can do the same when it comes to seeing the inner side of me. I like to have fun too, and sex with you helps me alleviate some of the stress I've been under, especially pertaining to Coach Johnson and my mother."

I knew how that was, and I leaned forward to join lips with Ms. Macklin. It was a lengthy kiss, too, but moments after, she got undressed and it was on. I let out the sofa and we got down on the springy, squeaking, thin mattress. It was so uncomfortable, but I could fuck Ms. Macklin anywhere and be satisfied. The same went for her, and after three orgasms that night, she was knocked out. I sat in a kitchen chair, staring at her from afar. I wondered where we would be in a year. There was something about my connection with her; I had never felt so attached to any chick like I was with her.

By morning, I had gotten back on the sleeper with Ms. Macklin and we were both knocked out. The bright-ass sun was shining through the window, and we couldn't help but keep tossing and turning from how uncomfortable the sleeper was. I held her close to my chest, and when she looked up at the sun, she dropped her head back down.

"You seriously need to get some curtains. What time is it?"

I looked at the clock that was hanging on the wall in the kitchen. "It's almost eleven o'clock. It's Saturday, and I hope you ain't got nothin' to do."

"I don't. All I want to do is lie in this bed and get some more rest."

She gave me a quick peck on the lips, and I couldn't be mad at her for stroking the shit out of my ego. I softly rubbed her back, occasionally massaging her ass.

"That feels so, so good," she mumbled. "I could lie here forever. Tomorrow, though, I have to go see about my mother. I promised her that I would bring her some new nightgowns, so do you want to go to the mall with me today to help me find her some?"

"No, thank you. I don't shop with women, but if you want to come back when you get finished, I'll be here waitin' for you."

She laughed and softly pecked my chest.

"Say, what's the story with your mother? You mentioned before that she was in a nursin' home, but is she that old?"

"She'll be forty-five years old this year. She's not old at all, but she has some mental problems. She needs around-the-clock care, and some days she's okay, but many days she's not. She hallucinates a lot and she's been diagnosed with being bipolar."

"I'm sorry to hear that. My mama got some issues too, and she just plain ol' crazy. You saw how she was in Mr. King's office that day, and that was just a sample of how she is."

Ms. Macklin laughed. "Yeah, she was quite a character. She was doing her best to protect you, though, and that was admirable. That's how my mother is, and when she's not going through one of her moods, she's really a beautiful person."

"What happened to her? I mean, was her problem hereditary or was it somethin' that just occurred?"

Ms. Macklin lifted her head and placed her chin on my chest so she could look up at me. Her eyes were so pretty, and I moved her hair away from them so I could see them.

"I'm not sure, Prince, but for years, my mother had been severely beaten by my father. It took a toll on her, and I can't tell you how many times I saw him beat her until she was unconscious. She was depressed all the time and it affected her. Growing up, I promised myself that I would never be with a man who put his hands on me. I don't want to wind up like her, and it is so gut-wrenching for me to see her in the condition that she's in."

I moved my head forward and kissed her forehead. "I know how that shit can be. My mama went through some of the same shit, and I ain't gon' lie when I say that shit fucked me up. I gotta get control of myself, and since I ain't never had no real daddy in my life, I'm tryin' to learn some shit on my own."

"I thought that was your father at the school that day. He was with you at the club that night, too, wasn't he?"

"That nigga ain't my old dude. That's my mama's on-again, off-again boyfriend. My father got killed, and I hate to say it, but when that shit happened, it was the best day of my life."

"Don't feel bad about saying it. I felt the same way; after what my father did to my mother, I jumped for joy when I found out he'd been killed. I didn't even go to his funeral, and if I had gone, I would have spit on him in his casket."

"Same here. Thing is, I thought about goin' to his funeral, just to make sure that he was on his way to hell."

"Me too," she laughed. "I know I shouldn't feel this way, Prince, but my father was really no good. He did a lot of people wrong, including me. It's because of him that I even started being a stripper. Whenever I'd ask him for money to help me and my mama out, he would tell me to get out and sell my body to get it. I had sex with some of his friends for money, and he even arranged it. He actually hooked me up with the man who owns the strip club I work for. Even though I hated to go that route, I felt as if I didn't have no choice."

"Damn, that's messed up. Yo' old dude sounds a lot like mine. I guess there's plenty of those kinds of niggas in the world."

"Yep, but there was only one Derrick Jackson. May that sucker rest with no peace."

My heart jumped and I quickly backed away from Ms. Macklin. "Wha . . . what in the fuck did you say your father's name was?"

"Derrick Jackson? Did you know him?"

Hell, nah, I thought. There were plenty of Derrick Jacksons in St. Louis, and there was no way in hell we had the same daddy. My palms started to sweat and I quickly sat up, moving farther away from her.

"When . . . when was your father killed?" I said in a panicky voice.

Ms. Macklin's forehead lined with wrinkles. She gave me a confused look, as she could see the concern in my eyes. "He was killed several months ago. They found his body behind a grocery store on Fifth Street. He was a notorious drug dealer, and was well known in the city. Like I asked, did you know him or something?"

I wanted to throw the fuck up! I jumped up from the sofa and went to do just that. As I leaned over the toilet coughing up nothing but mucus and spit, Ms. Macklin stood in the doorway with a sheet wrapped around her.

"Prince, what's the matter? Did . . . did I say something wrong? You know him, don't you? You were sellin' for him, weren't you?"

I wiped my mouth, and when she stepped into the bathroom and touched my back, I snatched away from her.

"Go put on your clothes," I yelled.

"Prince, what's wrong?"

"Do it!" I yelled. "Now!"

Her eyes watered and she walked away from the doorway. I stared at myself in the mirror, feeling as if that muthafucka was laughing at me, trying to get payback. Ms. Macklin didn't look anything like me, but her eyes, damn, there was something about her eyes. No wonder I felt so connected to her. I was mad as hell about this; all of this time I'd been fucking my own damn sister? When I thought about her being pregnant by me, I slammed my fist into the mirror and broke it. Glass shattered everywhere, and Ms. Macklin came back to the doorway. She was near tears.

"What is it?" she yelled out. "Please tell me. Why are you acting like this?"

I turned, looking at her naked body. How could it even turn me on at this point? Was I sick or what? *Damn*, I thought. *I'll be muthafuckin' damned!*

I wiped down my face and did my best to calm my voice. "Please put your clothes on. Please."

She stormed away from the door and plopped down on the sleeper sofa. Reaching for her clothes to put them on, she fussed and cussed her ass off.

"I am so fucking done with this," she said. "Fuck you, Prince. Here I am, pouring my damn heart out to you and you treat me like this? How dare you treat me like this? How dare you!" She was pissed, and even though I didn't want to tell her the truth, I had to. My emotions started to get the best of me too, as this was some fucked-up shit. I went over to her and took her hand. She snatched it away and stepped into one of her shoes.

"Leave me the fuck alone!" She stood up and pushed me backward. I didn't even trip, but then she smacked me. My head jerked to the side, and that's when I grabbed her arms and shook her.

"Goddamn it, Patrice! You're my fuckin' sister!" I yelled, then shoved her back on the sleeper. "Derrick was my damn daddy too!"

She looked like a mannequin posing, and didn't move. I wasn't even sure if she was breathing, and her mouth looked to be stuck wide open. "Wha . . . No, no, it couldn't be. Please. Why are you fucking with me, Prince? Don't mess with me like this."

I took a deep breath. My voice had calmed. "I wouldn't fuck with you like this. I wish like hell this was a joke, a dream, somethin'. But he was definitely my father. I don't understand how you didn't notice the resemblances. We look a lot alike."

Her eyes seemed to be searching me over, and that's when she covered her face with her hands. She broke down, crying and trembling so bad that I was afraid to touch her. I wanted to hug her or something, but that just didn't feel right to me. Instead, I sat next to her on the sleeper and hesitated before carefully rubbing her back.

"Don't . . . Please don't cry like that. I know this shit ain't good, but we didn't know. We gotta move on from this and . . ." I shrugged, having no damn answer to this myself. Ms. Macklin, Patrice, my sister, or whoever the fuck she was to me now, she dropped her head on my shoulder, continuing to let out her emotions. I dropped my head in shame as well, thinking about that no-good motherfucka that I had always known as my father. He sure as hell fucked us up, and I didn't know if Patrice or I would ever recover.

Chapter 16

The day I found out Ms. Macklin was my sister played out in my mind, every single day. We had kept in touch, and talked on the phone on a regular basis. She was in counseling and advised me to go with her. I just couldn't see myself spilling my guts to no stranger, so I told her she'd have to tackle that bullshit alone. The news about Derrick being father to both of us was hard to swallow, but we had to. My thoughts and visions about her had changed, and when we met up for lunch last weekend, the conversation was good.

I'd gone to see her mother at the nursing home, and as we sat in the room talking to her, I realized how much damage one single man had caused. There were so many lives fucked up, all because of Derrick. Patrice had been searching for love in all of the wrong places, and there was no surprise that she wound up falling for a brotha like me who was as close to her father as she could possibly get.

As for me, you already know my story. Maybe he could have made every bit of the difference in my life, who knows, but he wasn't willing to try. Mama had her faults too, and there was no excuse for her actions either. At this point, though, I wasn't trying to point the finger at anyone. Both of my parents lived their lives how they chose to, and now it was time for me to live mine. I complained about how they raised me, but if I wanted shit to change, I had to do better myself. Everywhere I went, I was paranoid about somebody finding out about what I had done to Derrick, or about killing Cedric. I didn't know if that shit was going to ever come back to haunt me, and my gut was telling me that it would. I got my ass off them streets, though, and was doing my best to live like a real street soldier.

No doubt, I had some work to do. What was gon' be, was gon' be. Patrice talked to me about getting my GED, and getting that was just one of my plans. I still hadn't gone to see about my son, and I was on my way to do that. Yeah, there was a possibility that I had more kids, but for now, I was taking this shit one day at a time. Monesha's son had been on my mind too, but I couldn't change years and years of what I'd been accustomed to overnight. Change took time. Someday, it would all work out for me, and deep down I knew it. I had some redeeming qualities, and my redemption started with today.

I knocked on the door at Nadine's house, nervous but knowing this was the right move. Lately, I couldn't stand that the son I definitely knew was mine would be without a father. I didn't want him to go through what I did, and if I could make his life better, I had to try.

"Can I help you?" Nadine's mother asked, as she came to the door.

"Is Nadine here?"

She gave me a puzzled look, then called for Nadine to come to the door. She did, and the baby was on her shoulder, covered in a blanket. A tiny smile covered her face, implying that she was possibly happy to see me. She stepped on the porch, and stood in front of me.

"All I can say is your mother is *crazy*," she said. "I've been trying to get in touch with you. Where have you been?"

I looked at the blue blanket covering the baby, ignoring what Nadine had asked. "What's his name?"

"What's yours?"

I smiled. "Let me see him."

She proudly turned him around, and his eyes were closed. He had a round face like mine, with chubby cute cheeks. His head was full of curly hair, and from the color of his smooth light brown skin, he damn sure didn't belong to no white boy, as I had assumed. I took him from Nadine's hands and held him in front of me. My palms were sweating and I hoped like hell he didn't slip. I eased down on the steps on the porch, still holding him at a distance. He squirmed around and pursed his lips like he was sucking on something.

"Be careful with him," Nadine said, sitting down next to me.

"I got him, ma."

I kept looking at him, seeing myself more and more. And when he opened his eyes, I damn near wanted to cry. Yeah, he was mine. And he was handsome as hell.

"And?" Nadine said. "I'm waiting."

"I wholeheartedly apologize for bein' an asshole. He mine, I know he mine. I wouldn't have this feelin' inside of me if he wasn't, and besides that, li'l man lookin' just like me, ain't he?"

Nadine rubbed his head. "Yeah, he got that fat head like yours," she said, then touched his nose. "And his nose is definitely yours. As much as I was mad at you, I knew he'd come out like this."

I put the baby on my shoulder, and his hair touching the side of my face felt like magic. He was so soft that I rubbed my face against his head. "I bet you ain't mad at me now, are you?" I asked.

"No, 'cause I love the hell out of my baby. I am, however, concerned about what I heard about you and Ms.

Macklin. Did you really go in the classroom and kiss her? I heard you'd been having sex with her, and I hope like hell that shit ain't true."

"Don't worry about Ms. Macklin. You need to only concern yourself with my baby, that's all. Are you back in school?"

"Yep. Mama been watching the baby, and I'm still gon' graduate on time. What about you? Are you coming back?"

"Nah, but I'm thinkin' about gettin' my GED. I gotta get a job so I can help you take care of my baby. Do you have any more of the money I gave to you?"

"Yeah, I got some of it left. I gave some to my mother to help her, but I got enough set aside for the baby. I'm thinking about going to a community college when I graduate, but I need to find me a job, too."

All I could say was it was a start. I had a feeling that my son was gon' change some things around for me, and I felt hyped about that.

Nadine and I sat on the porch talking for a while, and I suggested taking the baby to my mama's house so she could see him. At first, Nadine didn't want to go, but she changed her mind. When we got to Mama's house, this time she was in the kitchen, leaning against the counter while smoking a cigarette. We stood in the doorway with the baby, and all Mama did was stare. Her eyes did not blink until I introduced Nadine to her again. I removed the blanket from my son's head.

"This my son, Mama. His name is Prince. Jamal Prince Perkins, with a J.R. on it."

Mama blew the smoke from her mouth and put her hand on her hip. She then smashed the cigarette in an ashtray and walked up to us. She pulled the blanket back a bit more, and when Prince looked into her eyes, she did everything in her power not to smile.

"Yep," she admitted. "He yours. Look just like you when you were a baby, and I remember the first day when you came home from the hospital."

She carefully took him from my arms and we followed her into the living room. She sat on the couch with Prince on her shoulder, and leaned over to get a picture book from the middle of the table. She opened the book, and pointed to several pictures of me so Nadine could see them.

"See?" she said. "Look at this one here, Nadine. Prince was only a month old here, and on this one he was about three months old."

Nadine looked at the pictures and agreed that the baby looked just like me. Mama kept going on and on, and I was surprised when she turned her head to kiss his head. When he started to cry, she shook him in her arms and rubbed up and down his back. He quickly calmed down, and without paying me any attention, she didn't know I was watching the mother I had really and truly missed. My eyes watered a bit, but I blinked my tears away. I somewhat had memories of those days that she held me in her arms, rocking me to sleep. I wasn't sure what happened, but I contributed it to this thing called life.

Moments later, Raylo came through the door. He looked upset about something, and when Mama got after him about not coming into the house speaking, he started to go off.

"I speak when I want to speak," he fired back. "Don't be frontin' on me in front of no damn body."

"Fool, I was just tryin' to get you to show my new grandbaby some respect. Get that twisted-up look off your face and come over here and see him."

Raylo ignored her request. "Whatever," he said, throwing his hand back. "I know you'd better watch your damn tone with me, woman, or else."

"Or else what, Raylo? Take yo' ass back there and go to sleep or somethin'. Ain't nobody got time for your mess today."

"Fuck you," he spat.

"Nigga, fuck you!"

Some things were never gon' change. They kept at it, and as things got more heated, I took Prince from Mama's arms. I wasn't going to surround him with this kind of mess, and I knew damn well what being around it had done to me. I quickly got Prince the hell out of there, and Nadine and I went to my apartment to chill.

Prince Jr. was already five months old. We were at Nadine's graduation and we clapped as she walked across the stage to get her diploma. I was very happy for her. Even though I'd talked about getting my GED, that hadn't happened yet. I did have a job, though. Patrice had hooked me up with a manager she'd known at a worldwide package delivery service. He hired me, and I'd been driving a truck, delivering packages to businesses and residents throughout the metro area. The job came with good benefits and it helped with expenses for my son. On my off days, which were on weekends, Prince Jr. stayed with me. I was enjoying my new life. I'd never thought I'd be at a point where there was nothing but peace around me. Nadine and I were just doing okay. I hadn't even had sex with her since she'd had Prince Jr., and, truthfully, all I cared about was taking care of him. She wasn't happy about that, and had already started seeing someone else. I had no gripes, and the way I felt about females in general, it wasn't a good thing. No love for them was living in my heart, and I can't ever say that it ever was.

It was raining cats and dogs, muggy as ever. Nadine called, wanting me to take her to the Laundromat because she and Prince Jr. didn't have anything clean to wear. She was always bugging me about taking her places, and since she had my son, it was rare that I told her no. I carried her heavy loads of dirty laundry to my car. Moving aside two of my shirts and a pair of jeans on the back seat, I placed her baskets there and strapped Prince Jr. in the middle in his car seat. Nadine covered her head with an umbrella, but she got drenched when the umbrella blew up in the air. She hopped in the front seat of my car, soaking wet. I was too.

"Couldn't you have found a better time to go to the Laundromat?" I asked, wiping the rain off my face with my shirt.

"There was no better time. The meteorologist said it's going to be raining all day and I didn't have any clean clothes."

I pulled away from the curb, taking my time driving in the rain. "Why you didn't ask your boyfriend to come get you? That nigga ain't worth a damn, is he?"

"He had to work today, and you don't even know him like that to be passing judgment on him."

"I know he broke. And I know he ugly as hell. I do know that." I laughed.

Nadine folded her arms. "I know you ain't talking. You don't think I know about that old-ass neighbor of yours you've been fucking? She 'bout forty or fifty, which one?"

"Actually she's thirty-one, and how in the hell do you know who I've been diggin' into? You been watchin' me or somethin'?"

"No, but I just know these things. Every time I come over there, she be eyeballing me. I know what's up, and you can do so much better than that, can't you?"

I grabbed my goods and smiled. "Maybe so, but when she go down on me, she be treatin' this mutha like royalty. You ain't doin' it like that, so I had to move on."

Nadine shoved my shoulder, and when we got to a stoplight, she turned her head to look out of the partially lowered window. I looked in her direction too, and when a burgundy Regal pulled up beside us, my eyes stayed focused like a laser. The rear window slowly lowered and I saw the tip of an AK-47 aim in our direction. My foot hit the accelerator, but because of the wet pavement, all I heard were my wheels turning in circles, burning rubber. I yelled for Nadine to duck, and she dropped down on the front seat, yelling and screaming. "My baby!" she said. "I gotta get my baby!"

As the bullets hit my car, it sounded like a Fourth of July celebration going on. Glass was shattered everywhere, and, as fast as I was driving, the car beside us kept up. Nadine jumped up from the seat, shouting for her baby and trying to protect him. When her body jerked forward, I knew she had been hit by flying bullets. I slammed on the brakes, doing a spinning U-turn in the middle of the street that left my car smoking. Nadine's body fell backward, slamming into the dash and plopping down on the seat.

"Shit!" I shouted. I nervously touched her chest, trying to see if she was still breathing.

I couldn't believe this shit was happening, and as the other car sped away, I panicked, driving like a bat out of hell to get to Barnes Hospital, which was less than a mile away.

"Nadine!" I kept yelling, trying to get a response. "Get up!" By now, the whites of her eyes were showing and she had no response. From what I could see in the rearview mirror, Prince Jr. was okay. He sat quietly in the backseat, and I was thankful that the laundry baskets were on both sides of him. My breathing was getting heavier and heavier, my legs were shaking, and my sweaty palms were so slippery I could barely keep my hands on the steering wheel. When I reached the hospital, I put the car in park and carried Nadine's limp body into the emergency room.

"Help me!" I yelled at the nurses and doctors on duty. "Somebody please help me!"

My legs were weak as Nadine was taken from my arms and placed on a gurney. Her bloody arm flopped on the side, and the doctors and nurses rushed to get her into surgery. One of the nurses said that Nadine still had a pulse, and I was relieved to hear that. Blood was all over my soaking wet, rainy clothes that were clinging to my body. I'd seen who had tried to get at me. If you had ever in your life been robbed by a nigga, there was no way to forget his face. Thinking about my son, I rushed outside to get him from the backseat. Two nurses followed me.

"What happened?" one nurse said in a panic. "Please tell us what happened."

I couldn't even talk right now, and as I removed Prince Jr. from his car seat, I cuddled him in my arms. I felt his body for injuries, but he looked fine.

"Sir," one of the nurses said, now following me as I went back inside. "Do you mind telling—"

"Not now!" I yelled. "Please not now! Just . . . just make sure she lives, a'ight?"

The black nurse touched the other one's shoulder and looked at me. "We'll give you a few minutes, okay? But we really need to get some information from you. I know you're having a tough time, but I think you may want to get in touch with the young lady's parents."

I plopped down in a chair in the waiting room, wishing that this was all a bad dream. Nadine wasn't going to die on me, was she? Hell no! It wasn't going down like this, was it? I felt as if God had rarely come through for me before, but I needed Him to do it now! Tears fell from my eyes as I continued to rock my son in my arms, thankful that he and I both were okay. Maybe God had been looking out for me, but I needed an answered prayer like now!

Moments later, the black nurse came over to me, resting a blanket on my shoulders, trying to calm my chills. I got up enough courage to call Nadine's mother, but could barely get any words out of my mouth. When I told her Nadine had been shot, and what hospital she was at, her mother hung up on me. Right after my phone call to her, I called Mama. I didn't want to be alone. I just knew she was going to tell me that she didn't have time right now, so I was surprised when she said she was on her way.

So much pain was rushing through me, and I couldn't stop my heavy tears from flowing. Everybody in the waiting area was looking at me, and since I was shaking so badly, I laid Prince Jr. down in his pumpkin seat in front of me. He too started to cry, and when one of the nurses came over and reached down to touch him, I gripped her hand.

"Don't touch my fuckin' baby," I said through gritted teeth. "Leave us the hell alone."

The fire in my eyes implied that now wasn't the time to approach me, and she slowly backed away from me. It wasn't long before my mama came in, and Raylo was with her. She rushed over to me, picking up Prince Jr. to calm him.

"What in the hell happened?" she said, feeling my bloody shirt. "I thought you'd been shot."

I shielded my face with my hand, hiding my snotty nose and tearful, puffy eyes. "No, I said Nadine," I mumbled. "Some niggas were tryin' to kill me, but they shot Nadine."

"Oh my God," Mama said. "Was the baby in the car too?"

I nodded and she placed Prince Jr.'s head against her chest. When my head dropped, Raylo gripped my neck and massaged it. "Let it all out," he said. "Head up and we'll get them niggas, a'ight?"

That thought had already crossed my mind, and just when I thought I was getting on the right track. I knew my chickens would someday come home to roost, but never did I think it would come down to this. Nadine didn't deserve this, and if she was going to go out like this, somebody—a whole lot of people—would have to pay.

Nadine's mother rushed into the emergency entrance, asking the nurses behind the counter where she could find her daughter. The police were only seconds behind her, and we all turned our heads when two doctors came from behind the double wooden doors. Nadine's mother rushed up to them, as one removed a mask from his mouth and the other removed his gloves. The room fell silent, and I couldn't hear after I watched one doctor mouth the words, "I'm sorry."

From there, everything moved in slow motion. My watered-down eyes were so blurred, and all I could see was Nadine's mother yelling and screaming as she grabbed her stomach, squeezing it. She pounded her legs with her fists and pulled at her hair. The doctors, as well as the police officers, tried to get control of her. In a rage, she broke away from them and headed my way. The police chased after her, holding her arms from behind. From only a few feet away, she spat vicious words at me.

"You murderer!" she yelled. "How could you have done this to my daughter? *How?* I knew you were a no-good bastard, Prince! I warned her to stay away from your ass, and look at what you've done! Why! God, why? What did my child do to deserve this!"

She fell to her knees, and the whole place was at a standstill. Raylo kept massaging my neck, and Mama looked as if she was ready to cuss Nadine's mother out. As everything was spinning in circles, I jumped up from my seat. I ran past the police officers and Nadine's mother, who was unable to contain herself. Mama yelled out after me, and so did one of the police officers. He caught up with me just as I jumped into the front seat of my car.

"Calm down," he said, holding the door open. "We do need to talk to you, and if you don't feel up to it right now, then I ask that you come to the station tomorrow. If you don't, I will put a warrant out for your arrest. With all of these bullet holes in your car, I can only suspect what has happened. Remember, you don't want to bring no more trouble to yourself or to your family. Got it?"

I wiped my eyes and slowly nodded. The officer gave me his card and let go of the door. I slammed it shut and slowly drove off. I didn't give a fuck what he'd said. It had gone in one ear and out the other. Some people just didn't understand how or why shit had to go down like this, and even though I had made some progress over the last few months, a street soldier like me would forever have setbacks in the hood. No matter how hard I tried to do right, things would never work in my favor. Niggas were always gon' be niggas, thinking they could take a life without any repercussions. Not this time.

I knew exactly where Cedric and his crew hung out, but before I even got to my destination, I spotted the burgundy Regal parked in front of an auto body shop on the north side. Three of the niggas, including the one who had robbed me, stood outside laughing with the owner of the shop. They appeared to be having a funky good time, not even caring that a mother was somewhere grieving for her child. Yeah, it could have been my mama this time around, but to see Nadine's mother react the way she did was enough. I kept my eyes on the fools, making sure they didn't see me or my car. When they walked across the street to a lounge, I parked my car and changed my blood-soiled shirt with a clean one I'd had on the backseat. I waited for fifteen minutes, contemplating my next move. I thought about my son, living without a mother and father. Damn, I didn't want him being raised by Mama, and I knew that Nadine's mother was so upset with me that she'd probably want no part of him. Without me, he was guaranteed a fucked-up life. Maybe this wasn't the right thing to do, but when I looked at all of the dried blood splattered on my front seat, maybe it was necessary. As I was in thought, my cell phone rang. It was Patrice. I started not to answer my phone, but instead I did.

"Prince," she repeated, barely hearing my voice when I answered.

"What?"

"Why are you sounding like that?"

"Because I . . . I just wanna kill somebody right now, that's why."

"Who are you fighting with now? I hope you and your mother aren't at it again."

I wiped my tears, skeptical about telling her what had happened. "Nadine's dead. She got shot and I know the niggas who did it."

She hesitated to speak, but then spoke up. "I'm sorry to hear about Nadine, but you have to step back and let the police handle that. *Please.*"

"They ain't gon' handle shit and you know it. I'm gon' handle it, fa'sho."

"Go to the police now, Prince. This thing is much bigger than you. And, remember, it's up to you to change course. Millionaires are leaders, and followers like our father wind up dead or in jail. Don't be like Derrick, please. That's not what you want, is it? God said the vengeance is His—"

"Yeah, yeah, yeah, I got that. But today it may have to be mine."

I hung up on Patrice, only because I was being interrupted by numerous calls from Mama's phone.

"What?" I answered.

"Where are you?" she shouted.

"Out."

"Out where, Prince? Don't be out there doin' nothin' stupid. You need to get back here so you can see about your son. All this bullshit . . ." I heard Raylo saying something in the background, then he took the phone.

"He ain't tryin' to hear yo' goddamn mouth! Move back and silence yourself, woman. Young blood," he said. "Handle yo' business. That's what real niggas do, and make sure that whatever you do, don't you be the one leaving in no muthafuckin' body bag. Pump two for me. I expect to see you at your mama's house within the hour, pickin' up yo' son and goin' on with yo' life. Stay up."

Raylo hung up and I closed my eyes, listening to the many voices in my head. Sometimes decisions like this didn't come easy. People thought they did, but I didn't grow up saying that I wanted to be a murderer. But at this point, what choice did I have? All I can say is put yourself in my shoes. What in the fuck would you do? I heard Patrice pleading with me in her soft-spoken voice: *step back and let the police handle it. Please.*

Don't be like Derrick. Then Mama's voice got at me: *you need to get back here so you can see about your son.* Raylo: *handle yo' business. That's what real niggas do. Don't you leave that muthafucka in no body bag.* He sounded like the devil, making his noise, and I hated like hell to let the devil have his way. Then, there was another voice. It shouted so loud that my eyes popped open. *Vengeance is mine!* the powerful voice said. *All mine!*

Paranoid as hell, I looked around me. I thought about what Nadine's mother had said to me at the hospital, and wondered if she would ever forgive me. A vision of Nadine's lifeless body was in my head and that infuriated me more. *What in the hell would Romeo do in a situation like this?* I thought about how he'd been suckered by the white man, then about Nadine and her mother again. I shook my head, realizing how nobody understood how difficult it was being a street soldier at war. I had to not only do this shit for me, but for Nadine and her mother as well.

I tucked my silencer down inside my jeans, then put my five-inch blade in my pocket. I wasn't sure which one would come in handy first, but I knew both would be useful. I made my way toward the lounge, and could hear B.B. King singing the blues. I was careful about my surroundings, and when I entered the lounge, I found that the inside was pretty dim. Several people sat at tables talking, a few people sat at the long, red, painted bar, some were on the tiny wood dance floor, and I could see two of the brothas sitting at a table in the far back. The one who had robbed me had gotten up and was on his way to the bathroom. I lowered my cap on my head to cover my eyes. The other two brothas were busy talking, and as I made my way by them, they didn't even notice me. I entered the men's bath-

room, and leaned against the sink as ol' boy funked up the stall. No doubt, it would be the last shit he would ever take. Minutes later, he came out of the bathroom with his head lowered. He was buckling his belt, but when he looked up and saw me, his steps halted.

I smiled. "Say, nigga," I said with the sharp blade already in my hand. "You remember me?" He didn't say a word, and looked frozen in time. "Just in case you don't, I'm Prince. I'm here to tell you that your clock has stopped tickin'."

His beady eyes shifted to the door, and I could tell he was getting ready to jet. Before he could, I lunged out at him, shanking his ass with the sharp blade and jabbing it into his stomach. He staggered back, holding his ripped midsection. I pulled the knife out, only to jab it right back in four, five more times. I wanted his eyes to look like Nadine's did, and satisfaction came when he fell to his knees with blood gushing from his mouth. I wiped the bloody blade on his shoulder and watched his body hit the ground—hard.

Afterward, I retrieved the silencer from down inside of my pants, and left the bathroom. This time, I removed the cap from my head, just so the other two brothas could get a good look at me. I wasn't even sure if they recognized me, but they damn sure were introduced to my best friend. I shot off six bullets, instantly dropping those suckers like pesky flies.

The people in the lounge were clearing out fast, and backing away from me as if I was some type of madman.

"Oh my God," one lady shouted, falling over a table as she tried to break out toward the cluttered doorway. "He's got a gun!"

"Get Nay-Nay and them," another woman screamed at a man. "Lord, my daughter was back there in that bathroom! Get her!"

The man was too busy ducking underneath the tables, trying to hide, until I came into eye contact with him. He cautiously grinned at me. "Shut the hell up, bitch, and get yo' ass out of here! I'll go get her ass, but she shouldn't have been in there sucking dick!"

I couldn't help but snicker, as I'd sent the entire place into complete pandemonium. The people didn't know who was going to get shot next. As far as I was concerned, my mission was accomplished. Not quite, as I'd forgotten to put in two for Raylo. I turned, firing off two more shots that did nothing but get those fools to hell faster.

"Don't forget to say hello to the devil for me!" I said, smirking, with joy in my eyes. "That's if you mutha-fuckas can talk with all of those holes in dat ass!"

"He's crazy!" somebody shouted. "Call the goddamn police!"

That was my cue to jet, and as I rushed toward the door, everyone cleared out of my way. Some were falling, others hiding and shaking their heads. I figured a retaliation would be ordered, but there was no doubt in my mind that whenever that time came—today, tomorrow, whenever—I would ready. A street soldier such as myself always had to be.

Notes

Notes

Notes